I knew the form lying on the ground was a girl because that's what we'd been supposed to rescue; otherwise I might have hesitated before forming an opinion. There is a point in abuse and starvation beyond which the question of sex becomes meaningless.

"Can she walk?" I asked the woman tending her.

"I do not know. We carried her. We could find no shoes in the kennel where they had her. She was lying in filth, with only the rags you see. She only became truly conscious long enough to hand us the message. Even then she would not speak. Too much had been done to her, for her to speak."

A lot had been done to her, all right—and by the time El Fuerte and his men were through there wasn't much left of the girl with the code name of Sheila. There was just enough left of her to need me—to want me, to cling to me, to make me—Matt Helm—play God . . . and nearly get killed for my trouble.

the ambushers

by donald hamilton

An Original Gold Medal Book

GOLD MEDAL BOOKS

FAWCETT PUBLICATIONS, INC., GREENWICH, CONN.

MEMBER OF AMERICAN BOOK PUBLISHERS COUNCIL, INC.

I

THE NATIVES CALL IT the River of Goats, the *Rio de las Cabras*. In the time I was there I saw no goats, but that means nothing. I wasn't hunting goats, I was hunting a man. Anyway, we only ran up the stream a few miles, until the jungle started closing in on either side, overhanging the water blackly.

Then the Navy coxswain, who seemed to know where he was in spite of the darkness, put the junior-grade landing craft, if that's what you call it, in to the bank, and that was as far as I got to travel sitting down. I had the gun case between my knees so it wouldn't get knocked around or stepped on. The little pack, less sensitive, was down on the floorboards somewhere. I rose, kicked around, found it, struggled into it, and slung the long, heavy plastic case over my shoulder by its strap. I stepped ashore in the dark, hoping there wouldn't be any snakes or alligators to greet me.

Somebody said, "Good luck, sir. We'll be back the day after tomorrow."

The ugly little boat backed off silently—they've done some good work on mufflers since World War II—and turned sharply and hissed and burbled away into the night, heading for open water and the ship waiting offshore. There'd be coffee ready when they got aboard, I reflected. There's always coffee when you're with the Navy, but I wasn't with the Navy any longer.

There was nothing for me to do but stand and wait, so I stood and waited. I couldn't help thinking that there was a certain resemblance in names between the River of Goats, here in Costa Verde—well, let's call it Costa Verde—and the Bay of Pigs over in Cuba, where some other men had been put ashore not too long ago under somewhat similar circumstances. They'd been trying to start a revolution and I was supposed to stop one, but the basic situation was about the same. I couldn't help remembering that they hadn't had much luck at the Bay of Pigs.

Something rustled in the jungle behind me, but I didn't turn. I stood quite still on the river bank, letting whoever was there see me motionless against the dully gleaming water, with my hands empty. I didn't know how nervous he'd be.

"Senor Hernandez?" It was a soft whisper.

"I'm Miguel Hernandez," I said.

This was a lie. The blood of the *Conquistadores* does not flow in my veins. I was born in Minnesota, and while I moved to the state of New Mexico at an early age, and picked up a little Spanish there, I still get along better in some Nordic tongues, not to mention English. However, for this occasion, I'd had my face and hands stained and my hair dyed. I wasn't supposed to have to fool anybody up close. On the other hand, it was considered inadvisable to advertise too widely the fact that I was a foreigner. Besides, a dark face shows up less conspicuously in the forest.

"This way, senor," said the voice. "Follow me, *por favor*."

I turned deliberately and moved towards the sound. I saw a dim shape in the brush. There was a big hat and some more or less white clothing. The man moved off silently, and I followed the gleam of dirty white through the blackness, tripping over vines and getting the gun case hung up in tangled branches. Some people can take their jungles or leave them alone. I prefer to leave them, but I hadn't been asked.

We came into a clearing where a small fire burned. There were a lot of ragged, tough-looking, dark-faced men—about twenty, I judged—and a couple of ragged, full-bodied, dark-faced women dressed pretty much like the men, but you could tell the difference. I wondered briefly about the women; I hadn't expected any. I decided they'd been brought to make this bandit-looking crew look authentic. There were also a lot of firearms being treated in a very casual manner, including some nasty-looking little automatic weapons that caught the red of the firelight.

It used to be that a *pelado* with a machete was considered well-equipped, and if he had a rifle he was a great man. Now he's but nothing unless he's got a machine pistol that'll rip them off at the rate of several hundred rounds per minute. Well, the Latin temperament has never lent itself to careful, one-shot marksmanship. That's why I was there.

Of course, these weren't *pelados*. They had a trained, un-peasantlike look, and despite the presence of women, despite the nondescript clothes and casual manner, you could detect a military air about the encampment. My guide led me past the fire to where a man was sitting in a folding camp chair, smoking a cigar. He was a small, swarthy, mustached man in a big straw hat and soiled khakis. He needed a shave, and he was the type that misses the razor badly. Still, in some indefinable way, he managed to look quite jaunty and dapper in the flickering light. Perhaps it was the angle of the cigar that did it.

He was wearing a .45 automatic at his hip, in a military holster with a snap-down flap. If he'd locked it in his safe at headquarters, back in the capital city of Costa Verde—the saintly name of which escapes me momentarily—the weapon might have been a little harder to get at, but not much.

"The boat came, *mi coronel*," said my guide. "Here is the man."

The occupant of the chair dismissed him with a wave of the hand, watching me.

"You call yourself Hernandez?"

He hadn't risen to greet me, he didn't remove the cigar to talk, and his voice was curt. So it was going to be that kind of a job. I felt a surge of sympathy for the military gent, whoever he was, who said that he could deal with his enemies, but God would have to protect him from his allies.

"Who asks?" I demanded.

"I am Colonel Hector Jiminez." He pronounced it Himayness, Spanish fashion, with the accent on the second syllable.

"Then if you are Jiminez, I call myself Hernandez," I said.

"What is your true name?"

This wasn't really a state secret. The cover was primarily for his benefit, not mine. If he wanted me to break it, that was his business. It was his country and he'd have to live in it afterward. I wouldn't. Assuming, of course, that both of us survived the mission.

"My name is Helm," I said. "Matthew Helm."

He took the cigar out at last, looked at it, and threw it aside. He looked me up and down carefully.

"All this," he said, gesturing towards the fire and the group around it, "all this for just one man. All this merely to assist one long, clever gringo with a gun. Is that the gun?"

"Yes," I said. It didn't seem like the proper time to resent being called gringo.

"Show it to me."

"You'll see it when the time comes, Colonel," I said. "Not now."

His eyes narrowed. "It was an order, Senor Helm."

"And it was refused. With all due respect," I said. "The gun was prepared in a climate much dryer than this. It was enclosed in an airtight case with silica gel to maintain it at the proper humidity. To show it now would be to expose it to moisture prematurely."

He stared at me hard for almost a minute. Then he dropped his hand abruptly to the holster at his hip. If he wanted to get rough, I didn't have a chance, but I couldn't help putting my left hand—the right was grasping the rifle-case strap—on the butt of the little .38 on my belt, ready to twist it out of its trick spring holster. I guess I could have sold my life dearly, as the saying goes, but it wasn't exactly what I'd been sent there for.

Jiminez glanced at my hand, smiled faintly, and undid the flap of his big military holster with careful deliberation. He pulled out a fresh cigar. From another compartment inside the holster, he produced a tool with which to trim it and a lighter with which to light it. Then he returned the instruments to the holster and buttoned the flap down neatly.

"If I had been able to shoot as a junior officer," he said, blowing smoke at the nearby trees, "I would be a general now, Senor Helm. It is a great handicap to a military career, being a poor marksman. Since I cannot shoot, why should I burden myself with a big pistol?" He smiled a little. "Besides, if one has the firearms, one can always find men to use them. And even if one does not have them, generous friends will often supply them." He looked at the gun case significantly.

I drew a long breath. "I will open the case if you repeat the order, Colonel. But afterward I won't guarantee the results."

He nodded. "Very well. Get some sleep. It is not very practical to travel the jungle at night. In the morning we move."

"Yes, sir," I said, and started to turn away.

"Senor Helm."

I looked back. "Yes?"

"This silica of which you speak," he said curiously. "What is it?"

"It's a dessicant," I said. "Silica gel. It takes moisture out of the air. When it has absorbed all it can hold, you have to heat it in an oven to restore its efficiency. But we're not apt to be here long enough to make this necessary."

"No. We should reach the village of El Fuerte by tomorrow afternoon." He took the new cigar from his mouth and regarded it thoughtfully. "Silica gel. The wonders of North American science applied to the problems of Central American rebellion. Good night, Senor Helm."

II

FUERTE MEANS STRONG in Spanish, and it would make an interesting project for some statistically minded graduate student to determine just how many lawless gents have come out of those monkey-and-orchid jungles calling themselves El Fuerte, The Strong One. This particular contender for the strong-man title of Costa Verde was named Jorge Santos, pronounced Horgay. He was apparently doing well enough in a military way to worry the government of the country, not to mention some people in Washington.

"He's already got about a quarter of the country under his control," Mac had told me, briefing me on the assignment in his second-floor office in a shabby old building that isn't pointed out to visitors taking the standard rubberneck tour of the nation's capital. "Except for a few coastal plantations, it's the quarter nobody wants, but still it's real estate, and General Santos rules it in the name of the revolution. President Avila has asked the United States for help. For one reason and another, military intervention isn't feasible right now. We've been asked to do what we can."

I said, "Avila? Haven't I read something about President Avila of Costa Verde?"

"Probably," Mac said. The bright window behind him highlighted his clipped gray hair, but made his expression hard to read. "He is not the nicest friend we have down there. But his morals aren't the concern of this department, Eric, nor is the character of his government."

It was an official rebuke, emphasized by his use of my code name. He was reminding me that this wasn't the bureau of bleeding hearts. That was over in the State Department somewhere.

"No, sir," I said.

"The fact is, this Santos gentleman with the boastful nickname seems to have grown himself a beard like Castro and acquired the same kind of friends. The *Fidelista* movement seems to be quite contagious. Your contact will be a colonel in the Federal army named Jiminez. He'll arrange to get you in and out."

"Cheerfully?" I asked.

"Well," said Mac dryly, "they were apparently hoping for a couple of divisions of Marines. They may be a trifle disappointed. Furthermore, we have already made one attempt that failed. This will complicate your mission in several ways. . . ."

I thought of these complications now, lying with my eyes closed at the side of the jungle clearing. It was going to be a pleasant assignment, I reflected, with my target alerted and my allies disappointed and disillusioned, having already seen the job loused up once by an *Americano* miracle worker sent to take the place of the troops they'd requested. You could hardly blame Colonel Jiminez for being, let's say, a trifle reserved in his greeting.

It was getting towards morning, and the camp was starting to come awake after some hours of quiet, but I saw no reason to jump up and start functioning. There was nothing for me to do, and somebody might think I was too jittery to sleep. I lay there breathing evenly with my arm through the sling of the rifle case, until a man came to wake me and tell me that there was food by the fire and the colonel wished to inform me that we would march in ten minutes.

South of the Rio Grande—and we were a long way south—ten minutes usually means half an hour, but appar-

ently our diminutive C.O. wasn't one of the standard
mañana boys. In ten minutes we were on the trail, if you
could call it that, with daylight showing gray through the
tangled jungle. In fifteen minutes I was sweating copiously,
although the heat of the day was still to come. The little
man set a fast pace. I was in fair condition, but it wasn't
my kind of country, and the pathfinders out ahead were
picking holes for people their own size. Long-legged gringos
six feet four could damn well look out for themselves.

I stuck behind Jiminez, near the head of the column. He
never looked back. His faded shirt remained dry across
the shoulders. Behind me came the men who weren't swinging machetes out front, and the two women. I heard good-
natured grumbling in Spanish and deciphered some of it.
It was all very well for their *coronelcito* to amuse himself
by running the legs off the tall *Americano*, they were saying,
but he should take some thought to his own people, who
had marched hard yesterday and the day before. It was
not a joke worth killing oneself for.

If their little colonel heard them, you couldn't tell it
from his stride. He kept us as close to a lope as conditions
permitted, with only an occasional pause for breath and
food, and brought us to the outskirts of the village about
five in the afternoon, after circling wide to make the final
approach from inland.

At last I was told that our destination was just over
the ridge when we finally came to a halt in a wooded
ravine. We'd climbed all day, and this was a different,
higher, and dryer kind of forest from the jungle in which
we'd started, but it still wasn't likely to be mistaken for the
arid New Mexico country I'd hunted as a boy. The ravine
was apparently a prearranged rendezvous. A man was awaiting us among the trees, a barefoot peasant type in dirty
white pajamas and a big hat. Jiminez spoke to him briefly
in Spanish that was so different from my border lingo that
I couldn't really follow it. I gathered only that the man
came from the village, and that the situation there was
favorable in some respects, unfavorable in others.

The man slipped away. Jiminez got the two women and
three of the men off to one side and gave them instructions I couldn't hear. The older of the women carried a
machine pistol in a negligent manner. The younger packed
a rifle as if she knew what it was for. In pants, both
looked as tough as their male companions or tougher. I

wondered where all the gentle, shy, beautiful little Latin heroines were hiding, the ones who share the hero's bed, or bedroll, in every jungle epic ever written or filmed. Then I wondered what the hell I'd do with one if I had her. I wasn't exactly in the mood. I sat down on a log and rubbed my right thigh, from which a bullet had been extracted some months before.

"You have trouble with the leg, Senor Helm?" Jiminez asked, coming up to seat himself beside me.

"No trouble," I said. I couldn't have him thinking he had a cripple on his hands, on top of everything else, so I lied a little. "An old injury. It just stiffens up sometimes."

The mixed quintet, male and female, was moving off up the ravine. The older woman seemed to be in command. I assumed they'd been assigned to deal with one of the complications Mac had told me about. Jiminez caught the direction of my look and confirmed my thought.

"They will do what they can when the shooting starts," he said. "I do not have very great hopes for their success, however. There are at least two hundred men in the village, I have just been told. A few of those are paid by us, of course, but they cannot help openly or their usefulness is at an end."

"We're supposed to give it a try," I said. "But it's a secondary objective and they're your people. How hard you want them to try, under the circumstances, is for you to say. Is our primary objective at home?"

"Yes. I am told that he is expecting visitors by road before nightfall. We can hope that they will arrive before the light fails, and that he will come out of his hut to greet them. The entrance faces this way, as you will see when you get up there." He inclined his head towards the top of the ridge.

"Sure." I slid the pack off my back and got out the ten-power binoculars I'd brought along. "Will you assist me, Colonel, or can you assign me a man who speaks some English?"

"I will assist you personally."

It was good in some ways, bad in others. "It is understood," I said carefully, "that if I make requests or give instructions, I mean no disrespect for your rank."

He gave me his thin smile. He was a good-looking little man; he must have been a pretty boy. I didn't let that influence my judgement. Some of the meanest, switchblade-packing *pachucos* I'd known back home were real handsome kids.

He said, "It is understood."

"Then I want you to take these glasses," I said. "I want you to be watching through them when I fire. If I miss, you must tell me where it goes so I can correct the next shot properly."

"There will not be time for many shots," Jiminez said.

His expression didn't change, but it was clear nevertheless that he didn't like my talking about misses. One American agent had already missed.

I said, "If there's time for one, there's generally time for two. If I miss, look for the dust where it hits and give me the distance I'm off. In meters or fractions of a meter if you like. Give me the direction by the clock. Twelve o'clock, three o'clock, six o'clock, nine o'clock, or points between. You understand?"

"*Si.* I have shot at the targets, senor, if without much success. I understand. Just a moment."

He rose and spoke softly to a man standing by, who seemed to be a non-commissioned officer of some kind. The NCO went over to a group of others and spoke to them, pointing to the ridge. They all started scrambling upward, fanning out. Jiminez returned and sat down again.

"We will let them get into position and dig in," he said. "They will remain to cover us as we withdraw, as long as they can hold, outnumbered. Then they will retreat inland, while we hide overnight in a place that has been selected. If things go well, they will draw the pursuit after them and confuse it in the darkness, leaving us to make for the coast undisturbed tomorrow. It is a good plan, I think. Of course it will not work."

I glanced at him quickly. "Why not?"

He shrugged his shoulders. "No battle plan has worked in every detail since the dawn of history, senor. Why should this one?" He glanced at his watch. "We should take our positions within ten minutes. We must be ready when the visitors arrive."

"Sure."

I reached for the plastic case and pulled the long zipper and broke the seal inside. I suppose it was a solemn moment, kind of like finally consummating the marriage after a long courtship. Well, the real consummation was still to come, but I'd spent a long time preparing this equipment and bringing it here; just taking it out should have been celebrated with a little ceremony, say a toast or a prayer. However, it was no time to be drinking, and I've kind of got out of the habit of praying. I just reached in first and found a little bag containing what looked like white gravel and tossed it to Jiminez.

"There's your silica gel, Colonel," I said.

Then I took the big rifle out of the case. It was a heavy match barrel on the long Mauser action, shooting a hand-loaded version of the .300 Holland and Holland Magnum cartridge that I'd cooked up myself. I slipped off the rubber bands and removed the corrugated cardboard that gave additional protection to the scope, a twenty-power Herrlitz. We'd used European components for the same reason that I'd dyed my hair and called myself Hernandez. American interference is kind of unpopular down there and tends to bring unpopularity on the party that requests it. If we were killed or caught, there wasn't supposed to be too much Yankee debris left lying around.

The stock was a plain, straight-grained hunk of walnut without much sex appeal, but it was fitted to the barrel and action with artistry. A regular G.I. leather sling completed the outfit.

It was quiet in the ravine as I got ready, except for an occasional murmur of conversation among the five men who remained with us, and an occasional rustle or scuffle from above, where the men who were to protect our retreat and lead off the pursuit were getting set for phase one of their suicide assignment. I was glad I wasn't the one who'd had to give those orders; on the other hand, I couldn't help remembering that I was the one who had to make all risks and losses worthwhile. If I fluffed my part, as my predecessor had done, a lot of men might die here for nothing. Well, that wasn't anything it would help to think about.

I saw the colonel pick up the case I'd dropped and slip the bag of silica gel back inside, closing the zipper. He looked at the gun I held.

"It is an impressive firearm," he said.

"Let us hope the man we came to impress finds it so," I said.

He glanced at me sharply and started to speak, but checked himself and was silent, watching while I rigged the rifle sling for shooting, and dug one box of cartridges out of the pack. They were big, fat shells. They looked as if an ordinary service round had had a clandestine affair with some anti-aircraft ammo. I could only get four of them into the gun: three in the magazine and one in the chamber. I stuck the box in my pocket and closed up the pack.

"Well, Colonel?" I said. "Let's look the situation over."

He hesitated. "You do not seem very confident, Senor Helm. You have some reservations?"

"What do you want me to do, claim the turkey before the target's been scored? You want some shooting done, it says here. Or your president does. Let's go."

He did not move at once. I could see what he was thinking. He had no faith in me, and he was thinking that he was still not fully committed. He could still pull out, or try. He might get away; he might even make it back to the coast undetected, with his task group intact. As for the inefficient *Americano,* he would of course have to die so that he could not tell what had happened—in a brush with El Fuerte's men, the report would state regretfully. It would be a very fine report, full of heroism and courage, the kind you send in to excuse a failure. With the American dead, who could contradict it except General Jorge Santos, who wouldn't be asked?

All this went through his mind; then he shrugged and reached for my pack. "You want this brought, I suppose. I will carry it. Follow me."

With the big rifle heavy in my hand, I followed him up through the brush. Below us, in response to a signal he gave as he passed, the five men in the ravine were picking up their weapons and drifting up into cover after us. I guess they constituted our mobile reserve, or something. The little man trotted up the slope at a slant, and I made my long-legged way after him, until he flattened out near the top and waved me down. We crawled the rest of the way.

A man lay behind the rock up there with a carbine. It was the NCO. He had several extra clips arranged in front of him. We crawled into a bush to his left and looked out.

It was worse than I'd expected. There was a road down the cleared valley below. I guess they grew some kind of corn there, but I never got close enough to be sure. The road was the usual two wagon ruts. Well down along it was the village. The huts weren't much, mainly roofs thatched with some kind of leaves, supported by walls that looked insubstantial and drafty, but the housing standards of rural Costa Verde weren't my concern, and in that climate I guess you generally don't need much more than a roof, anyway.

The place was full of men. They had several fires going. There were women among them. There were a great many weapons in evidence. That wasn't my concern, either. At least it wasn't supposed to be. The military aspects of the situation were the colonel's worry. What did concern me was the fact that the nearest hut was at least a quarter of a mile away. I spoke softly without looking at the little man lying beside me.

"Which one?"

"It is the third hut along the road, on the left. The third from this end. Of course, when he emerges, he may come this way."

"And he may go the other, too," I said. "It depends where the damn visitors decide to stop. I was told the range would be approximately three hundred and fifty meters. Three hundred and eighty yards." He did not speak. Still looking down the valley at the distant huts, I collected some saliva in my mouth and expelled it on the ground in front of me. "To use a phrase from your language, Colonel, I spit on your lousy three hundred and fifty meters, sir. Give me that pack."

"Senor Helm—"

"Just give me the damn pack. Let's see what we've actually got here. There's no chance of getting closer, I suppose? What about that point of woods down to the right?"

"There is an outpost right below it. There are patrols. It was determined that the thing would have to be done from here."

"Sure. Three hundred and fifty meters away. You grow damn long meters in this country, Colonel Jiminez."

I pulled the pack in front of me for a rest and laid the rifle across it. I had to hunt a bit to pick up my target—those big target scopes have a narrow field—then the third hut was clear and sharp in the glass, but it still wasn't exactly at arm's length. It was going to be one hell of a shot, if I made it.

I LAY THERE TELLING MYSELF hopefully that at least the wind wasn't blowing. As I watched through the scope, a man walked into the field of the instrument from the right and entered the hut, walking right through the scale and crosshairs. A moment later he reappeared, leaving, but stopped in the doorway, apparently addressed by someone inside. He answered respectfully, saluted clumsily, and walked out of the scope.

"Five hundred and fifty yards," I said. "Approximately. That, Colonel, is over five hundred of your meters. Your informant was damn near fifty per cent off."

"You can read the distance?" He sounded more interested than apologetic.

"There is a scale inside the telescope," I said. "You take a man like that one, approximately five and a half feet tall—at least I hope he wasn't a pygmy or a giant—and you place the lowest division of the scale at his feet and read the range opposite the top of his head, making allowance for the sombrero. Then you take this figure and enter the table I have attached to the stock of the rifle, here. You learn that to hit a target five hundred and fifty yards away, the way this particular rifle is sighted at this particular time, you must hold over eighteen inches. In other words, I will have to shoot for the top of the head to hit the chest."

Actually, of course, I hadn't ever believed their story of three hundred and fifty meters. I'd sighted in the rifle at four hundred and fifty yards, and run my compensation table from three to six hundred, just in case. There has seldom been a spy yet, or a hunting guide for that matter, who wouldn't underestimate a range badly. You always hope the day will come when somebody will hand you the straight dope, but a fifty per cent error wasn't much more than par for the course.

"That is truly scientific," Jiminez said. I couldn't tell whether he was being ironic or not.

"Sure," I said. "It assumes I can find a man the right size to take the range from, and that he's standing up straight, and that I'm not looking at him from too great an angle up or down. It assumes the gun is shooting where it was when I made up the table, a few thousand miles away in a different climate. And at five hundred meters, Colonel, it takes this bullet the better part of a second to reach its target. A running man can cover thirty feet in one second. You'd better pray the guy stands still for us. What do you want me to do afterward?"

"Afterward?"

"Do we pick up and run for it, or do we try to give your boys a hand in stopping the first rush?"

"That is for you to say, Senor Helm. I cannot ask you—"

"If you don't ask," I said, "who will? I'm sure as hell not volunteering; I gave that up when I got old enough to vote, or a little before. But El Fuerte's men have got an open valley to cross, and I've got sixty rounds of ammunition nobody told me I had to bring home. Once we're back in the woods, this gun is useless. With a twenty-power scope, it's got to be shot from a rest; it's no good for jungle fighting. But right here I might do some good, if I'm so ordered by my commanding officer, in this case you."

He hesitated and looked at me for a moment. He laughed softly. "Very well. It is an order. Senor Helm?"

"Yes, Colonel."

"It is sometimes hard for men of different languages to understand each other. I may owe you an apology. I—"

He stopped abruptly, and picked up my binoculars, hanging from their strap around his neck. He crawled forward to focus them on the road where it came into sight below and to the left of our position on the ridge. I heard it now, the sound of a motorized vehicle approaching from up the valley. Well, that wasn't anything I needed to look at.

I took off my hat quickly, and dumped the contents of the open box of cartridges into it, and set it where I could reach it easily. I took the other two boxes out of the pack and set them beside it. I closed up the pack again and replaced it to support the gun, and settled myself comfortably behind it. Then I made sure, by counting huts —one, two, three—that I was looking at the right one through the telescopic sight. With high magnifications at long ranges, it's very easy to find yourself watching the wrong door or window, or even, if they're all similar, the wrong house.

I shoved off the safety and double-checked, by looking, that it was really all the way off. That's another mistake that's been made by people who should have known better, including me.

"Colonel."

"Yes, senor."

"The hell with the jeep or whatever it is. Watch the doorway. Confirm the identification fast when he shows. And you'd better slide back a bit if you value your eardrums. This thing is loud."

Then it was just a matter of waiting. I'm not an iron man; I had the usual quota of palpitation and perspiration. I resisted the temptation to turn my head to watch the progress of the jeep down the valley. One glance had told me it was a jeep, with a native driver and a man in sun helmet and khakis, who looked too tall and blond to be indigenous. That was all the glances I had to spare. I lay there forcing my body to relax along the ground. I was just an eye at the ocular, a finger on the trigger. A man went into the hut to announce the impending arrival and emerged. A moment later another man came into sight in the doorway.

He didn't come all the way out right away. He had to tease us. He stopped in the shadow of the door to put on his uniform cap. The sunlight was bright on his thick body from the waist down, but the rest was in shade. I couldn't be sure of my crosshairs and I hadn't got an identification from Jiminez, anyway. I resisted the urge to ask a silly question. He'd speak when he was sure.

The man took a step forward, and another—and kept walking. My mind went through the calculation rapidly. At two miles per hour, he would move a couple of feet in the time it took the bullet to reach him. If I allowed for his motion, he could stop and it would strike ahead of him. He could speed up and it would strike behind.

"Shoot," said Jiminez softly. "That is El Fuerte. Shoot!"

I'd worked too hard and come too far to risk my first shot at that range, on a moving target. He was a big man, I saw, not tall but broad and solid, with the shoulders and arms of a gorilla. He had a scraggy, Castro-type beard, but he was a far cry from the lanky Castro type, physically speaking. El Fuerte, The Strong One. He was dressed in suntans, with that uniform cap. General Jorge Santos, pronounced Heneral

Horgay Santos. He stopped at the side of the road to wait for the oncoming jeep. A couple of his men came up to wait beside him, one directly in the line of fire.

I could feel the sweat trickling down my face as I lay there, waiting. I heard Jiminez stir impatiently beside me, but he had sense enough to keep his trap shut. Five hundred meters away, General Jorge Santos took one step forward into the clear and turned to look up the road toward us. The crosshairs settled on the fancy insignia on the uniform cap, a tiny, gleaming aiming point so far away. I wasn't aware of adding the last fraction of an ounce to the pressure already on the trigger, but the big rifle fired.

It made a hell of a noise in the quiet valley; it was like setting off a cannon-cracker in church. It slammed back against my shoulder and cheek. It's not a fun gun to shoot.

"Call it," I said, working the bolt fast and trying to pick up my target again in that lousy scope. "Call it, damn you!"

"He is hit," Jiminez said calmly. "He is going down."

Then I had my man back in the field. El Fuerte was being supported by his two companions, but his knees were buckling and there was blood on his shirt. His head was hanging and his cap had fallen off. I gave it the same rough eighteen inches of Kentucky elevation and fired again. There was the same damn volcanic eruption and the same piledriver blow against my face and shoulder.

"Bueno," Jiminez said in his calm voice, but he'd forgotten to speak English. *"Muy bueno! Uno mas?"*

He was asking for one more, the bloodthirsty little bastard. I yanked the bolt back and slammed it home again, but there were more men around Santos now, and as I waited for a clear opening, the jeep drove up and stopped, blocking my view completely. I looked up. The whole village was stirring, but they didn't really know what was going on. The thunderous report of the Magnum would have sounded vague and directionless down there, like distant blasting. At that range you can shoot at a deer all day, if you're that bad a shot, and he'll never even stop browsing until you land one close.

"Shoot again!" Jiminez hissed. "Shoot at anything. Our people will have heard. They will be entering the village. You must make a diversion."

I had my eye at the scope again. Since the target didn't matter, I took the most conspicuous one. I picked up the man in the sun helmet standing in the jeep, and fired, but he was already going to the ground in a long leap as the

Magnum roared, and I knew I'd shot behind. When I picked him up again, he was flat on the ground with a silly little pistol in his hand. I could see his face clearly.

It was kind of a shock, because it was a face I'd seen before somewhere, although I couldn't put a name to it. It was a German face, a Prussian face, the kind that goes with a monocle, a shaved head, no neck, and sometimes an honorable Heidelberg scar across the cheek. With the sun helmet on him, at the angle I had, I couldn't be sure of the neck or the haircut, but the scar was there all right. If there was a monocle, it was in his pocket.

The pistol was a Luger, I thought. With that face, it would have to be a Luger. They'd liked Lugers better than the new-fangled P-38s that shot the same cartridge; and they'd liked riding quirts and polished boots; and they'd thought they could use Hitler to do their dirty work for them, but he'd fooled them and made them do his dirty work for him, instead.

And what was a man like that doing in the Costa Verde jungle, visiting a bunch of Spanish-speaking revolutionaries? The answer was easy. Anywhere else a man like that was apt to die, legally or illegally, at the hands of people who still remembered various things that had happened during World War II. It was a long time to hold a grudge, as far as I was concerned, but then I didn't have the motives some folks had.

I'd hesitated a moment, looking hard at the face, trying to recall the name; and the moment was too long. He'd been sniped at before, and he knew the crosshairs were on him. He crawled under the jeep. I let him go.

"El Fuerte is finished," Jiminez reported. "Very good work, senor. Now to the right. To the right of the nearest hut fifty meters. Keep those three men from reaching the forest or we will be outflanked too soon."

They had my gun located now. The last shot had done it. A bareheaded character with long, wild black hair and waving arms had rounded up half a dozen armed men in the street and was shooing them toward us. More were running to join him. To hell with him and his charge of the light brigade up the valley of death. The automatic weapons could deal with the problem when the time came. But off to the right, a quieter type with a machine pistol was leading a couple of cronies with rifles up the slope for an end run.

I led him like an antelope and knocked him over. His pals flattened out in the grass.

"Keep your eye on that pair while I reload," I said. "Keep them located for me."

From there on in it was a real wild party. At least I found it so, but you must understand it was new to me. I never fought in the South Pacific jungles; I never even fought in Europe, to call it fighting. We operated there, and we killed people and got shot at, sometimes, but it wasn't war, our part of it, although war was going on all around us.

This was war—on a small scale, of course, but how big a piece does the average soldier get to see? We had all the war we could handle, anyway, and I reloaded and picked off the two men where Jiminez pointed them out, first one and then the other, as they showed themselves.

"*Bueno,*" he said. "Just a moment, Senor Helm, please."

I looked his way, and he was cutting off a cigar and lighting it. Then he closed up his damn cigar-case holster, settled down comfortably on his elbows, and put the binoculars to his eyes again, blowing smoke in a satisfied way.

"The second hut," he said. "On the left. There is a group forming. Put a bullet through it about half a meter from the left corner. . . . I am sorry, senor. I am rude. Do you wish a cigar?"

"Thanks, I don't smoke," I said. "Thanks just the same."

I put a bullet about half a meter from the corner of the hut, and after that I put a lot of bullets in a lot of other places, and people, as he directed in his unruffled voice. They formed in the village and started up the valley to avenge their general under the leadership of the long-haired guy. At Jiminez' word, I shot the long-haired guy at four hundred yards, and another man took his place, and I shot him at three hundred, holding under a bit, but they kept coming, crawling, running, darting from rock to rock and bush to bush, squirming through the corn or whatever it was.

When they got within reach of the short-range weapons, Jiminez took the cigar out of his mouth deliberately. He blew a little whistle he fished out of the neck of his shirt on a cord, and everything on the ridge opened up. The racket was impressive. All we needed was some heavy stuff to have a real battle. I shot a charging man so close that I had nothing but his shirt in the twenty-power scope; I could see the coarse weave of the cloth.

It was time to reload again, but they were falling back and I had trouble getting the shells into the gun without scorching my fingers. Besides, it wasn't my picnic any more. The machine-pistol and carbine boys could handle it from here. Jiminez tapped me on the shoulder as I closed the bolt. I looked up to see the younger of the two women squatting beside us, heedless of the stuff that was going through the trees around us. There was blood on her sleeve and she had her hand tucked into the front of her shirt to keep the arm from flopping around, but she wasn't paying any attention to that, either. They were a hell of a bunch of people. There's nothing like a pro, in any line of work.

"She says the secondary mission was successful," Jiminez reported. "The prisoner was released, with the loss of one man. There is a message for you. Here."

It was a sliver of wood, or reed, with a hard yellowish surface like bamboo. Maybe it was bamboo. I'm not an expert on the flora of the region. On it a pin or tack had scratched a line of shaky capital letters: INVESTIGATE SOMETHING BIG DOWN ROAD PAST VILLAGE SHEILA.

I looked at Jiminez. "What is the condition of the prisoner?"

He shrugged. "What can you expect? It has been over a month, almost six weeks. It is a miracle she is still alive. What about this?"

"I'd like to take a look," I said. "If it's important enough for her to make the effort to tell us, in the shape she's probably in, it's important enough for us to look at."

"We are through here anyway," Jiminez said. "The rest is routine. The corporal has his orders. He will pull back when he is outflanked and lead them away inland. We will go investigate this big thing."

IV

IT WASN'T SO BIG. It wasn't as tall as the Washington Monument by any means. Hell, you could have hidden it in an ordinary farm silo, if you could have figured a way to slip it inside. It wasn't nearly as big as the ones they play with at

Cape Canaveral. Still, it wasn't something you'd take home on the Fourth of July and set off in the back yard to amuse the kiddies. Coming on it cold in a well-guarded clearing in the Costa Verde jungle, I found it impressive enough.

It looked a good deal like a gigantic version of my .300 Magnum cartridge, standing there, except that it wasn't brass. They'd given it a fancy coat of camouflage paint to make it harder to spot from the air. But there was the same fat body necked down to the same slim, pointed, bullet-shaped head—the warhead, I suppose. I studied that carefully. Washington would want to know whether it was nuclear or otherwise. I didn't have enough technical knowledge to tell, but maybe I could spot some detail that would tell somebody else.

They had a net suspended over it covered with leaves and stuff. Farther back along the edge of the little jungle opening was the truck, also with camouflage paint and a net. It was a six-wheeled tractor with power to all three axles and a big cab, like the ones the non-stop cross-country truckers sleep in. But I didn't think the extra space housed a bunk in this case. There were a couple of trick antennas, and I could make out the corner of some kind of a console or control board through the open door.

Behind the tractor was the long flat trailer with a cradle to hold the bird and hydraulic equipment to set it up. It was a real little mobile, do-it-yourself missile base. There was painted-over lettering embossed on the truck that I couldn't decipher, neither English nor Spanish. Not only the language but the alphabet was different. Even at the distance, I didn't have much doubt as to what language it was. But the two bearded men squatting beside the truck as if they belonged to it weren't Slavic types.

"May I look?" Jiminez whispered.

I'd taken back my binoculars earlier. I passed them to him again and watched him adjust them to his eyes, lying beside me in the brush. I couldn't read his expression. I looked around the clearing. They had a couple of heavy machine guns set up strategically—there had been one nest along the road that we'd bypassed—and there were too many nervous sentries pacing around nursing too many rapid-fire weapons to make an attack seem like more than a forlorn hope. Just to get the two of us this close to the barbed wire undetected had taken all the woodcraft both of us possessed.

A fresh burst of firing inland indicated that Jiminez' boys were still leading the paper chase away from us. The men in the clearing looked that way, grimly or uneasily according to temperament. They knew the village had been hit; they were expecting to be next.

"Cubans," Jiminez whispered. "Those two by the truck. With the beards. One supposes they are technicians lent by Castro to his fond *amigo,* General Santos."

"Along with a nice little Russian toy that somehow got side-tracked when they were all being shipped home as a result of the U.S. blockade of Castro's island. I wonder what Khrushchev said when his inventory added up one whiz-bang short?" I grimaced. "How did they get it in here?"

"They could have floated it up the river and landed it well above where you were set ashore. There are little-used roads by which a truck like that, assisted by men with axes and shovels, could have brought it the rest of the way. It would take much work but it could be done. Senor Helm?"

"Yes?"

"I am not well acquainted with such weapons. What would be the range of this one?"

"I'm no expert, either," I said. "But I should think it would shoot at least five hundred miles. Our Polaris goes well over a thousand and it's small enough to fit on board a submarine crosswise."

"It would seem, then, that we reached El Fuerte just in time," whispered Jiminez, still studying the missile grimly. "With this, if it is as powerful as one suspects, he could have blackmailed our government into submission. Our capital city is less than three hundred of your miles from here. He could have threatened to destroy it if their demands were refused." After a moment, the Colonel said, "I will have to speak to my informants in the village. They should have learned of this."

I said carefully, "I am thinking, Colonel, that my government would be pleased if something happened to that thing."

He lowered the binoculars and turned his head to look at me. "I know you are thinking that, Senor Helm," he whispered. "I am thinking what *my* government would wish me to do. Now that El Fuerte is dead and the revolution no longer has a leader, I am not certain they would wish it damaged. A thing like that has many uses, in the proper hands." He moved his shoulders. "But we speak of what is impossible. Those men are alerted. We cannot take them by surprise, and we have not enough force to overwhelm them. No. It is my duty to report this. That is all I can do. Come."

It was no place to argue; and even after we'd extricated ourselves from there, I wasn't in a very good position for argument, deep in an officially friendly country surrounded by well-equipped representatives of its armed forces. Anyway, stray missiles weren't really in my line. I'd done my work and, like Jiminez, I'd make my report. Washington could take it from there.

We rejoined the rest of our group and reached the hiding place while the light still held, though it was fading fast. Two of the men of the special contingent that had entered the village, and the older woman—the younger one, wounded, had remained with us after delivering the message— were awaiting us in a grove of trees that seemed too dense for a snake to penetrate. But there was a way in, and in the center was a space like a good-sized room, a kind of arboreal cave.

I left Jiminez posting sentries and went over to the woman who sat at the side of the space watching over a strange girl lying on the ground. I knew it was a girl because that's what we'd been supposed to rescue; otherwise I might have hesitated before forming an opinion. There is a point in abuse and starvation beyond which the question of sex becomes meaningless. The woman looked up.

"She took a little food," she said in English. "Now she is asleep. Do not wake her unless it is necessary."

I didn't comment on her knowledge of the language. "Can she walk?" I asked.

"I do not know. We carried her. She would have cut her feet to pieces, since we could find no shoes in the kennel where they had her. She was lying in filth, with only the rags you see. She only became truly conscious long enough to give us the message on the piece of wood. Even then she would not speak. Too much had been done to her, for her to speak." Anger stirred in the woman's face. "El Fuerte and his men are beasts, senor."

"His men may still be beasts," I said. "El Fuerte is nothing, now. Not with two 180-grain slugs through the chest."

The thought had not really pleased me before. I mean, there had been nothing personal between me and General Jorge Santos when I shot him. But as I knelt beside the unconscious figure on the ground, I took some pleasure in the fact that I hadn't missed.

It wasn't pretty. I knew that our agent who went by the code name Sheila, although I had never seen her before, was normally a rather attractive young woman twenty-six years old. She'd gone to good schools. She'd been married and divorced before she joined the outfit for reasons that were not recorded. According to her dossier, she was five feet two inches tall, weighed a hundred and fifteen pounds, and had gray eyes and shoulder-length brown hair bleached and tinted to gold for this assignment—blondes are rare and conspicuous down there, and she had wanted to be sure of catching General Santos' masculine attention, which rumor said wasn't hard to catch.

At last report she'd vanished into the jungle in a jeep with a native driver known to be favorable to the revolution. She'd been carrying a bag of cameras and a tape recorder, and she'd been posing as a leftist girl journalist doing a story on the heroes of the revolution, in a deliberately provocative blouse and intentionally tight Capri pants.

It was supposed to be the old Delilah routine. If everything had worked out, sooner or later she'd have been found standing over General Santos' dead body with his smoking army pistol in her hand, clutching some torn lingerie to her bosom and weeping hysterically. The Federal informers in the village had been alerted to protect her from too-drastic reprisals; in the disorganization that was expected to follow Santos' death they were to have smuggled her out to safety. If this had worked, I'd never have been called upon to help make up a sniper's rifle capable of dropping the general in his tracks at three hundred and fifty meters or maybe a little more.

Everything had not worked out for Sheila. Things had gone very wrong, we didn't yet know how or why. But she'd obviously been detected and caught somehow; she'd apparently paid most of the usual penalties; and now after a month and a half there was hardly enough left of the carefully planned blouse-and-pants costume to qualify as clothing— and there wasn't a great deal left of the girl who had selected and worn it, either. The starved, scarecrow figure on the ground before me, rags and dirt included, didn't weigh more than eighty pounds.

They'd hacked off most of the phony-gold hair, dark and matted now, with a bayonet or machete, I suppose as a mark

of shame; and they'd done something to the left hand. It was
wrapped in some stained and grimy cloth that might once
have been part of a feminine garment of silk or nylon. I
looked at the hand and at the dark-faced woman. She
moved her shoulders matter-of-factly.

"They tried to make her talk, to name her accomplices in
the village, senor."

"Did she?"

"Would we have risked our lives for her if she had?" As I
reached out to examine the hand and arm, the woman spoke
quickly: "Do not touch her, senor."

"Why not?"

"You are a man."

She said it as if it explained everything, and I guess it did.
I looked at her for a moment, and she looked right back. She
was actually a rather handsome woman, I noted, in a
solid, swarthy, and savage way. I gathered she didn't think
much of men. At the moment I wasn't too fond of them
myself.

"Sure," I said. I took off the pack and opened it, kneeling
there. "Well, she's going to have to swallow her natural
and justified prejudice against the sex, just for a moment. I
don't like the looks of that arm. I want to get some penicillin
into her right away."

"I will give the penicillin. I have done it before. She will
scream and fight, perhaps harm herself, if you touch her. We
had great trouble bringing her away."

"All right," I said. "I leave her in your care. Here are the
clothes I packed in for her. If you need any help, let me
know."

The woman didn't answer. Her attitude said that when she
asked any man for help, that would truly be the day. Well,
her psychological quirks were no problems of mine, thank
God.

I left the stuff with her and went over to Jiminez, who
was in a fine lousy mood, too, maybe because he couldn't
smoke his cigars in here without possibly betraying our
hiding place, maybe because we could still hear sporadic
firing back in the hills where his men were letting themselves be hunted through the growing darkness to save our
skins. Or maybe he had other things on his mind, missiles
for instance. Anyway, his small, dark, handsome face didn't
light up noticeably with friendship when I came up.

"How is she?" he asked curtly.

I moved my shoulders. "I'm afraid it's going to be a job for the doctors and psychiatrists. All we can do is bring the pieces home. Maybe they can put them back together. If not, well, we have a place for people who didn't make it. The problem arises fairly often in our business."

"You take the ruin of a lovely girl, your associate, very calmly." His voice was cold. I couldn't see that the comment required an answer, so I didn't speak. He said, "But then you are proud and happy tonight, Senor Helm. You were brave today. You shot with great precision. You killed many men."

"After you'd spotted them for me," I pointed out. After seeing Sheila, I wasn't in the best of moods myself.

He drew a long breath. "Yes, that is true. I helped."

"Are you grieving for Santos, Colonel?"

"Bah!" he said. "El Fuerte was a pig. But his men. . . . Did you see them come, senor? Their leader was dead, but other leaders rose among them. We shot those, and still they came, right up to the guns. . . . President Avila would execute them all for rebels and bandits. In this country, you understand, a rebel is a bandit always. And El Fuerte was truly a bandit. But there are times when I remember that those are my people, too—yes, even the ones who did that to your female agent. After all, she came among them to deceive and kill. They had some provocation, senor. Perhaps one day they will find a leader worthy of them. In the meantime—" He grimaced. "In the meantime, I help gringos shoot them down at five hundred meters. You will excuse me. I mean no offense. But I do not like to see brave men die." He hesitated. "One favor, Senor Helm."

"It is granted," I said formally.

"The gun. The big rifle. I am sure our President would like to see it, the gun that killed El Fuerte half a kilometer away. May I take it to him?"

"Sure," I said. After all, it was government property. I had no further use for it, and I was sure that a gift to cement inter-American relations would meet with official approval. "Sure. Take it. On one condition."

"And that is?"

"That you or one of your men carry the heavy old bastard out of here. It almost broke my back on the way up."

He laughed quickly, and we were friends again, or as

close as we were likely to come with our different back-grounds.

"You are *muy hombre*, Senor Helm," he said. "If there have been misunderstandings, I apologize. You are much man."

I said, "Good night, Colonel. It's too bad you couldn't learn to shoot as a junior officer. I think you'd have made a swell general."

In the morning everything was quiet. We started down the hill, carrying Sheila on an improvised stretcher, since she proved incapable of making it under her own power. In the late afternoon, without incident, we reached the river. In the evening, the landing craft came along to pick us up and take us downstream and out to the ship.

It was a practically perfect operation in every respect, I thought. Two days later I was in Washington learning otherwise.

V

AFTER A WEEK OF IT, I wasn't very eager to get back to the second-floor office on Monday morning and find out from Mac what else I'd done wrong, so I did my duty and visited the recognition room in the basement, as we're supposed to do whenever we're in Washington. I went through the files, refreshing my memory about the people in our line of business considered important enough to be given a certain priority. I read up on Dickman, Holz, Rosloff, Vadya, and Basil, all nice people who'd kill you as soon as look at you.

There were some old names missing, the ones we'd caught up with here and there or somebody had; and there were some new ones who'd just graduated to priority status. Reading about their latest accomplishments made me feel much better. It was like reading about old friends getting up in the world. These were people you could count on, unlike the supercilious sons of bitches in the Pentagon and State Department and elsewhere in this lousy town that had probably been a fine swamp before some fool decided to drain it.

Mac didn't disappoint me. He had a new list of criticisms some bright lad in spats had thought up on the golf course over the weekend. Well, I guess I'm being unfair. I don't believe they really play golf in spats. I stood at the window and looked down at the sunlit street, listening. The girls walking past below looked fresh and pretty in their gay summer dresses or tight, bright pants. They were probably nice enough girls, I reflected. It was unreasonable to dislike them because they'd never seen a man killed, or a woman broken by brutality and systematic degradation.

I said without turning my head, "Goddamn it, sir, if it was intelligence they wanted, why the hell didn't they apply to the CIA? I went down there to shoot, not to take notes and photographs. Have they made up their minds what we're dealing with yet?"

Mac rustled some papers on his desk. "Your description apparently fits the Rudovic III or IV," he said. "That is a miniaturized version of the other side's best intermediate range ballistic missile with some very interesting developments that give it almost the range of the larger prototype. The differences between the two models are internal, affecting the propulsion system and the type of solid fuel used. The later model has a range of some sixteen hundred miles, according to our best information, which isn't very good. The previous model was supposed to have a twelve-hundred-mile range. It is probable, but not certain, that it was the older Model III that was lent to Castro, one of which he hid out and passed on, perhaps to get it off his hands before his Russian friends learned about it."

I said, "It doesn't much matter which one. Neither could hit the U.S. from down there. But there's always the little ditch known as the Panama Canal, which is within range of both."

"Precisely," Mac said. "A lot of the details of the mobile Rudovic system are still unknown here, but it has been definitely established that all models use nuclear warheads. Here in Washington it is generally referred to as the Moscow Mite."

"It may look small from Washington," I said. "It doesn't look so damn small when you see it from a bunch of jungle ferns just outside the barbed wire. Is there any word from President Avila yet?"

Mac said, "The president is very busy with military affairs. Following the success of a daring raiding party that attacked the rebel headquarters and killed the bandit leader Santos, we are told, Federal troops have advanced into the area and are busy mopping up the disorganized remnants of the self-styled revolutionary army. As soon as the situation is stabilized, says the Ministry of State, a thorough investigation will be made." Mac paused deliberately. "There is still some feeling here in Washington that it would have been very nice if you could have settled the matter while you were on the spot."

"So they're still on that kick." I turned to look at him. "Which officious jackass, of the dozens I've met lately, made the suggestion this time?"

"The comment was made in conference Friday night. The name of the commentator will remain confidential. I pointed out that you had a specified assignment and carried it out brilliantly. Without specifying the nature of the assignment, of course." Our duties are not supposed to be common knowledge, even among the higher circles of Washington officialdom.

"Thank you, sir," I said. "I suppose they think I should have stuck it in my pocket and brought it home for them to look at. Hell, it only weighs what? Five tons? Ten tons?"

Mac said, "Well, there is no doubt that a sample of the Rudovic, any model, would be gratefully received. However, I doubt anybody really feels you were in a position to supply one."

"Maybe they can get it out of President Avila."

Mac said dryly, "The president of Costa Verde is our great friend and a true democratic leader of his people, to be sure. Still, I doubt anybody here wants to see him get his hands on a nuclear weapon. Nor does anybody have great hope that if he does get his hands on it he will turn it over to us."

"I see," I said. "So I'm the patsy. Well, I could have died heroically shooting thirty-caliber holes in that overgrown firecracker, I suppose. Since I don't have any idea where the thing keeps its brains, the chances of my doing any real damage would have been slight. And I'd probably have had to murder a Costa Verde Colonel to do that much."

"Ah, yes," Mac said. "Your friend Hector. I can never pronounce that last name."

"Their jays are aitches, sir. The accent is on the second syllable. Himayness."

"A short evaluation of Colonel Jiminez is desired by the military." Mac reached out and flipped a switch. "We are recording now. Subject Jiminez. Proceed."

"His men refer to him as *El Coronelcito*," I said. "That is an affectionate diminutive meaning The Little Colonel. Any resemblance to Shirley Temple is probably accidental."

"Shirley Temple?"

"There was a movie, 'The Little Colonel', from a book by the same name. Or a series of books. For girls."

"Indeed? Go on."

"The most significant thing about Jiminez, I think, is that when informed he was to rescue a woman prisoner, he brought two women along without being asked. I don't believe they were part of the normal task group organization, although they certainly pulled their weight right along with the men. I think Jiminez just figured our girl, if still alive, was apt to be in pretty bad shape and would prefer female attendants in her misery. Of course he was perfectly right." I paused. "This guy has got something. I think it's called compassion, but don't transcribe that. It's not something I'm an expert on myself."

Mac said, "I don't think our military planners are interested in his compassion, Eric."

"Then they're making a bad mistake," I said. "Because Hector's compassion is very interesting, and he's apt to make general yet. He's a good man. He's not a softy, you understand. Physically, he's a pretty little fellow in excellent condition who smokes big cigars that he keeps in a pistol holster. He threw away the pistol because he couldn't hit anything with it, he says. He'll stop to light up in the middle of a fire fight. Latin bravado, sure, but it's reassuring to the troops. You figure, if he can put on a show without even a gun to shoot back with, so damn well can you. In action, I'd trust him all the way as long as our objectives were identical, but no further. Where politics are concerned, I wouldn't turn my back on him for a fraction of a second. He's got deep thoughts, our little colonel has. I wouldn't want to say what's at the bottom of them."

"And Avila? Was he discussed?"

"*El Presidente* was barely mentioned in conversation. Jiminez indicates he's bitter against the rebels and would like to stand them all up against a wall and use them for machine-gun practice. It looks as if he might get his chance. Well, that's a normal presidential attitude down there, I guess. Or anywhere."

"End of recording on Jiminez and Avila," Mac said, and pressed the switch again. He looked up. "That brings us to the mysterious visitor in the sun helmet. We've finally managed to dig up some pictures for you." He pressed a button and spoke into the intercom; he was getting gadgety as hell, I reflected. He said, "Would you bring in the photographs, Ellen? And pick up a tape for transcription?"

We waited in silence, until a pretty girl came in with a manila envelope which she laid on the desk. She was wearing a blue dress and high-heeled blue pumps, and her pale blonde hair was soft and shiny. It wasn't fair of me to resent her. She was well trained, I knew—they all are in that office—and because she had access to certain information she carried a small capsule hidden somewhere on her person. One day she might have to take it, or worse, she might not have time to take it. That day just hadn't come yet, for her.

She smiled at us, extracted a small reel of tape from the recorder built into the desk, and went out without speaking. Mac opened the envelope and drew out a thick sheaf of photographs, holding them out to me. I took them and sat down to go through them. You wouldn't believe how many scarred Germanic characters there are in the world. We seemed to have pictures of most of them.

I was aware of Mac shifting positions in his chair as I approached the bottom of the pile. Then the man in the sun helmet was looking at me from a glossy print, with the stern, martial expression of any army officer posing for an official photograph, which this was. It was a German Army photo, and the man was wearing a general's uniform. The uniform brought it back.

"Von Sachs," I said without looking at the identifying caption. "Heinrich von Sachs." I looked quickly at Mac. "You knew?"

"I was fairly sure from your description. I wanted you to pick him out yourself. You remember him now?"

"Yes, sir. He's damn close to the top of the list, now they've got Eichmann, isn't he?"

"Very close. The difference is that Eichmann, when captured, was no longer actively dangerous. He was simply hiding out, trying to preserve his life. Von Sachs is a different breed altogether."

"Sure." I looked at the scarred, rather handsome face in the photograph. The face I'd seen through the telescopic sight had been older and grimmer, but then, whose wasn't? I said, "I guess he called himself a patriot. Maybe he still does. Maybe he is one. He just had a nasty way of showing it. They had him running the slaughter pens for a while, to keep him in line, didn't they? But they had to give him back his command eventually. In a military way, he was a good guy to have around, I guess, if you didn't mind your victories liberally seasoned with atrocity. And that wasn't something that kept Hitler up nights, as I recall."

"We are not concerned with his atrocities except indirectly," Mac said rather reprovingly. I remembered that he had always worked on the theory that we were a practical organization—a tactical organization—and that the sword of retribution was not our weapon. He had never accepted an assignment that involved killing a man just because he was a louse, perhaps because once you get into that racket it's so hard to know where to stop. "Nevertheless," he said, "when you took that shot at von Sachs, it's too bad you missed."

I looked at him across the desk. I laid the pictures gently before him and rose and went to the window.

"My apologies, sir," I said. "It was an oversight. The next time I will mow down everybody in sight, just in case there's somebody on the premises somebody wants dead."

"Eric—"

"I will also," I said harshly, "be careful to carry enough explosive to blow up any installation of military value anybody might possibly want destroyed. I regret I did such a sloppy job, sir. I am terribly sorry I simply knocked off the guy I was sent to knock off. If you will give me another chance, sir, I promise it won't happen again."

He said, "Sit down, Eric."

"Just tell me one thing, sir," I said. "Is there anything or anybody else I carelessly neglected to destroy or assassinate down there? I like to get all my reprimands in one package."

"It was not a reprimand," Mac said. He watched me go back to the chair. What's the matter with your leg?"

"Nothing," I said. "It's still a little stiff, is all. That Jiminez set one hell of a pace going in; and then I helped

carry the litter coming out. Like a damn fool I'd got rid
of everything else I was packing, so I was the logical candidate for one end of the thing. I've still got blisters on
my hands. If it's not a reprimand, what is it?"

"I merely said it is too bad you missed," he said, "because I'm afraid I must ask you to repair the error. We've
been asked to deal with von Sachs. I had another agent
scheduled for the job, but he has never seen Heinrich
in the flesh. You have, now."

I said, "It would have been nice if I'd known this when
I had the guy in my sights. And I don't like being credited
with an error, sir, when I'm only firing to make noise because somebody's asked me to."

He said, "You are very touchy today, Eric."

I said, "It was a good, clean operation. And ever since
I got back people have been climbing all over me because
I didn't do a lot of things that weren't in the orders." I
grimaced. "Skip it. Von Sachs is the subject. Elaborate."

"We could hardly warn you to look out for him in
Costa Verde, since we had no idea he was going there and
still don't know why he went. It's rather peculiar, as a
mattter of fact. Politically, he couldn't have had much in
common with General Santos; you might say he's at the
other end of the political spectrum. He has been operating,
according to our sketchy information, in northern Mexico
and across the border in southwestern United States, trying
to establish a variation of the usual Nazi-Fascist program
that has gained some adherents farther south in this hemi-
sphere, Argentina for instance."

"I'll bet his variation is a cute one," I said. "He was a
great little hater back in the forties, and he's had lots of
time to practice since. From what I saw, I'd say some kind
of a Latin-American deal was being cooked up regardless;
El Fuerte was giving him the VIP treatment. This leftist-
rightist stuff doesn't keep the boys apart when there's a
mutual advantage to be gained by getting together. Well,
that particular axis never got established. Probably it's just
as well."

"Probably." Mac frowned. "There is an added complication you had better know about. Von Sachs is still being
sought by certain groups interested in bringing him to justice
for his older crimes. We may sympathize with their objectives, but we do not approve of anybody's circumventing
our extradition laws and treaties, or those of our neighbors,

by extra-legal means. That is what I meant when I said that his atrocities concern us indirectly."

"I see," I said. I looked at him for a moment. "What you mean, sir, is that nobody's going to embarrass anybody's government by putting the international snatch on a dead war criminal."

"Precisely," Mac said. "I want you to drive out to the ranch and have Dr. Stern, or his assistant, take a look at that leg. That will put you right in the area. The materials and instructions are not quite ready yet. I will have them sent out while you are en route."

VI

THE RANCH IS IN SOUTHERN ARIZONA. To get to it, you drive first to Tucson and check with a certain telephone number, after which you proceed out of town by a specified route, seldom twice the same. Presently you pass a man changing the tire of a pickup truck or filling the radiator of a jeep or just standing beside an out-of-state sedan to snap a picture. If the door of the vehicle has been left open, you can go ahead. If it's closed, that means somebody's tailing you, and you have to go back to Tucson and await instructions.

The ranch is sanctuary—for some, a next-to-final sanctuary. It is the one place in the world an agent can relax without worrying who's behind him. Like most Nirvanas, it has its drawbacks, but it's safe; and every effort is made to keep it that way.

We got the all-clear signal on the first try and kept going. I had my fingers crossed. The car they'd wished off on me was a tremendous old Pontiac station wagon, built in the days when station wagons were still being made of wood. Now, sixty-odd non-stop hours out of Washington, D.C.—well, I'd occasionally napped on the front seat for an hour or so—it was banging along on only five cylinders and three wheels, or at least that was my impression. It didn't have to be correct. After wrestling the brute for twenty-four hundred miles, I wasn't as sensitive to impres-

38 DONALD HAMILTON

sions as I might have been. The only thing that could really impress me, at this point, was a bed. I hoped no last-minute breakdown would keep me from it.

The gate looked like any ranch gate in that country. It had a cattle guard and the usual friendly ranch-country sign: POSTED, NO TRESPASSING, NO HUNTING, NO WOOD HAULING. From there, the dirt road went back into the desert for five miles. Here was another gate, not a cattle guard this time, but a real, swinging-type gate with another sign reading: PRIVATE PROPERTY—NO TRESPASSING. I got the ancient mechanical monster stopped with some difficulty—the brakes weren't behaving right, either—and stumbled out, hoping the poor old beast wouldn't die while my back was turned. Idling, it sounded very sick indeed.

I got the gate open, remembering how it was supposed to be done, which wasn't the way you'd normally open a ranch gate. This told the gent watching through binoculars from somewhere up on the nearby hogback that it was okay not to shoot me. I drove through, limped back to shut the gate in a specified way, got back into the wagon, and drove on. After another two miles, the road dipped down into a green valley, and there was the ranch, a great, sprawling adobe structure in a grove of cottonwoods.

It had once been a guest ranch that went broke. Now it's supposed to be the property of a rich old crackpot with religious notions who's often visited by friends as looney as he is. Well, that's pretty close, except for the religious angle. Actually, the place belongs to rich old Uncle Sam, and I guess we qualify as his friends, and if we weren't crazy we wouldn't be in this business. I eased the old heap down the hill on what compression was left in the remaining cylinders, and let it roll to a stop in the yard.

We were expected. A man in a sports shirt was coming to meet us. The doctors don't wear white coats at the ranch, and the nurses don't wear uniforms, but they aren't hard to spot.

"You can wake up any time," I said over my shoulder. "We're in."

I heard my passenger stir in back. The guy in the bright shirt came up. He was young and earnest-looking, with metal-rimmed glasses, and he had all the qualifications of a good doctor except common sense and a sense of humor —well, any kind of sense at all, to be perfectly honest.

That's just one man's opinion, of course, based on previous visits.

He was one of the first-name boys. He was Dr. Thomas Stern, and he ran the place with all kinds of authority, but he'd think you were mad at him unless you called him Tom.

"Hello, Tom," I said. "She's in back. Give her a chance to put her shoes on."

"How's she feeling?"

"I'm just the chauffeur," I said. "I'm just the guy who gave her a lift because we happened to be going the same way. Telepathy is out of my line. . . . No, I wouldn't go back there and get helpful."

He'd started toward the rear of the wagon. He stopped, frowning. "Why not, Eric?"

"Get a nurse, anything in skirts," I said. "She's gotten kind of used to me, to the point of silent toleration, but I don't know how she'd react to you." I limped around to the rear of the wagon and yanked open the transom and dropped the tailgate. "All right, Skinny," I said. "Out you come."

The thin little girl sitting on the blankets in the rear of the station wagon looked a lot more human than the one I'd helped lug out of the Costa Verde jungle, but she wasn't a jewel of glowing health and perfect adjustment. She just stared at me silently and crawled back to the opening, waiting for me to get well off to one side before she swung her legs over and slid to the ground.

She was wearing a pair of slim, tapering cotton pants, light tan in color, and a boy's white short-sleeved shirt. They'd been clean and crisp enough in Washington, D.C., but now they looked kind of like a well-slept-in suit of pajamas. Well, I was in no position to criticize. My costume was no fresher. At least she didn't have a beard.

I'd been feeding her milkshakes and stuff clear across the country, whenever she was awake enough to absorb nourishment, but she still hardly cast a shadow. Her left hand was still wrapped in bandages. Her face was all bones and eyes, mostly eyes. Her hair had reverted to a light shade of brown, like the description in the files, and the machete haircut had been repaired as far as possible. Actually, it didn't look much worse than the short tousled messes some girls pay money to wear on their heads, even in this era of haystacks and beehives.

But it was the eyes that got you. They were big and gray and shiny, and sometimes they were big and yellow and shiny, and they never seemed to close at all. They were watching all the time, waiting for something dreadful to happen.

"She's all yours," I said to Dr. Stern. "So long, Skinny. Thanks for the company, such as it was."

I saw the eyes change, just a little. I was getting to her. If I'd had her for another sixty hours, I might even have made her blink. Dr. Stern was looking at me reproachfully. He obviously thought I lacked tact and feeling. A stout nurse in a print dress was glaring at me.

"Oh, you poor little thing" she said to the girl, putting her arm defensively around the narrow shoulders. "Come on, honey, this way. You're just going to love it here. You'll see."

I could feel the eyes following me as I went to the front of the car to get my hat off the seat. Then the nurse was leading her away. I felt a little funny about it, almost as if I were going to miss her. I'd carried her feet twelve miles through the jungle; I'd driven all of her twenty-four hundred miles. She had still to say a word to me, but I guess you get used to having somebody around even if you mustn't touch them and they won't talk.

"The materials you're to study arrived yesterday by air. They're in your room," Tom Stern was saying. "But you'd better come into the office first. We're supposed to take a look at that leg."

"The hell with the leg," I said. "Just point me at a bed and stand back out of the way."

"Well, in the morning then," he said. "You're to call Washington when you've done your homework. What do you want done with the car?"

Sheila was just disappearing into the building, a wraith in pants beside the husky nurse in her print dress. I've never been able to work up a great deal of interest in trousered women, but then, she wasn't really a woman, just a pair of yellow-gray eyes. I looked at the Pontiac and shook my head regretfully.

"You'd better shoot it," I said. "It isn't humane to let it suffer so."

I followed one of the houseboys into the building. Two people were sitting in wheelchairs on the veranda or, as they call it in that country, *portal*, with the accent on the last syllable. The man had only half a face, acid had got the rest. The woman looked all right, but I knew, because I'd seen her on a previous trip when I came out for special training, that she'd sit there without moving until they brought her in and fed her and put her to bed. Her eyes didn't bother me much. They were just dead.

These were people who'd made the same mistake Sheila had: they'd got caught, somewhere, by somebody. And if you think mixing up the permanent invalids with the agents in for retraining or repairs, like me, was just an accident or an economy measure, think again. We were supposed to see them sitting there, the ones who hadn't quite made it. It was a gentle reminder of what happened when you goofed. As I say, the place is safe, but it has drawbacks.

I had a nice big room with a desk. There was a lot of stuff on the desk. I started opening the packages and said to hell with that. And to hell with the fact that there was still daylight at the window. I pulled down the blind, undressed, got into bed, and went to sleep.

VII

THE THING WAS wearing drifting white robes and stretching out its white arms to me and whispering my name. I couldn't see its face clearly. I tried to wake up and found that I was awake. That didn't seem right, somehow. Apparations ought to stick to dreams where they belong.

It was still there in the middle of the room, illuminated only by the kickback of the yard lights outside, as much as could penetrate the drawn blinds. I'd been sleeping heavily a moment before, and I wasn't thinking very lucidly, I guess. I just knew that I didn't believe in ghosts, and that I had no midnight mistresses in the place, and that tricks were sometimes played here in the name of training and analysis, to see how fast you could react.

I went for the white thing before it could come for me. I lunged out of bed low, cut it down, wrapped it up, and pinned it to the floor. It was dressed in some material that was coarse to the touch; the idea of a shroud came to mind. The hell with that. Somebody was playing games, and they could damn well go play them somewhere else. Then I felt the weak, panicky struggles and heard the frightened breathing and I knew at last what I had. I let go and got up and turned on the light, feeling foolish and angry.

"Jesus Christ, Skinny," I said. "Don't tell me you walk in your sleep on top of everything else."

She was huddled on the floor, kind of tangled in a Navajo rug. I thought she was crying, but the face she turned up to me was dry. The eyes were dry. They were perfectly enormous, and the odd yellow light was in them. She shrank away as I stepped forward to help her rise. I stopped.

"Relax," I said disgustedly. "I figure a hundred pounds for the legal raping size. You're still safe by at least ten pounds. What the hell are you doing here, anyway?"

She didn't answer, of course. I went over to my suitcase, found the sandals and dressing gown I hadn't bothered to unpack earlier, and put them on. When I turned again, she was standing up. They'd given her some kind of a crude, straight, sleeveless cotton gown that reached the floor. So much for my dream of drifting robes. It wasn't the sexiest garment in the world, but it had a kind of convent simplicity that went well with the thin face and the big eyes and the chopped-off hair. She could have been a martyr on the way to the bonfire.

She said, "Don't leave me here."

I stared at her for a moment. It was a perfectly good human voice. Well, I should have known she had one somewhere.

"Please don't leave me here," she said clearly.

I drew a long breath. "I haven't the slightest intention of leaving you here," I said. "This happens to be my room and I'm still way behind in my sleep. I'm booting you out into the hall this minute, unless you come up with a very good reason to the contrary, fast."

"I mean this place. I don't want to stay here."

"Why not?"

The big eyes watched me, but they were no longer yellow. They only went yellow when she was scared or mad, I decided. These were gray eyes. If they'd only blinked occasionally, they would have been nice sensible eyes. When she spoke, her voice was quite sensible, too.

"Don't be silly," she said. "It's a glorified funny farm, that's why not! And I'm the newest, cutest inmate, and I'm just going to love it here if they have to kill me to make me. Well, I don't love it! I think it's perfectly horrible. Everybody feels so goddamn sorry for me, except you!"

The blasphemous adjective went oddly with her saintly, ascetic appearance, barefooted in the rough white nightie.

"What makes you think I'm not sorry for you?" I asked, startled.

She said, "Because I know perfectly well you think I'm a clumsy little idiot who caused everybody a lot of trouble by botching up a perfectly simple job and getting caught so some people had to get shot rescuing her and others had to get blisters on their hands carting her to safety!" She got it all out in one rush of words while I stared at her. Then she said, "Of course, you're perfectly right."

I didn't know what to say to that. She watched me unblinkingly, waiting. It was funny—in a sense I'd known her for well over a week, but she hadn't really been a person until this moment. She'd just been some damaged government property for which I'd been more or less responsible, off and on. And now that she'd become a person, she wasn't at all the person I'd expected. Before either of us spoke, there were footsteps in the hall.

"There's a light," said the voice of the big nurse I'd seen earlier.

"Please!" Sheila hesitated and stepped forward quickly. It was obviously the bravest thing she'd done in her life, but she managed to force herself to touch me, to take my hand gingerly and turn it over so the half-healed blisters showed. She looked up at my face and whispered, "Please! Why did you bother to carry me out of the jungle, if you were just going to leave me in a dreadful place like this?"

Then they were at the door, and she let go my hand and shrank back guiltily, as if caught committing a monstrous perversion.

"Oh, there you are, honey," said the big nurse. "Don't you know you had us all worried, disappearing like that?"

She was an imposing figure in a striped seersucker dressing gown, with her hair in curlers. She'd apparently been called out of bed by the night nurse, a stout little woman trying to disguise her profession in a costume of brightly printed shirt and shorts.

"We're a naughty girl," said the smaller woman. "We promised nursie we'd go right to sleep."

"Don't scold her, Jonesy. It's hard the first night in a strange place, isn't it, honey?" The big nurse smiled brightly. "We know you didn't mean to cause trouble, dearie. You were just looking for a familiar face, weren't you, honey? Now you come with us and we'll give you something to make you sleep."

She gave me a hard look that said I hadn't heard the end of this. They all went out of the room. Sheila never looked my way. I didn't sleep as well the second half of the night as I had the first; in fact, after a while I got up again and went through the stuff on the desk. In the morning I reported to the office according to instructions.

The orthopedic surgeon they had in the place—Stern wasn't a scalpel-type doctor—was named Jake Lister. He was about six feet tall and about six feet wide and he'd played pro football to pay for his medical education. He had big white teeth in a black face, and long black fingers that could be gentle and sensitive as a musician's, but weren't always.

"Ouch!" I said. "Why don't you just pull it off and take it over to the lab for examination? I'll wait here, holding a hanky over the bloody stump."

Lister grinned and straightened up. "Nothing wrong with you that a little exercise won't cure, man. You've been sitting on your behind too much, that's your trouble." He went on to prescribe a series of squat-downs and push-ups to be performed, it seemed, continuously day and night.

"That's fine," I said. "When do I sleep and eat?"

"Ah, hell," he said. "Why do I waste my breath? Any time one of you sinister characters gets a little seniority, he's suddenly too proud to do simple exercises. I tell you what, you go over to the gym three times a day as long as you're here and have the Dago give you an hour's workout with the foils or sabers. No epée, mind you, that's too precise and static. The hell with form. Just mix it up fast and sloppy. If Martinelli's busy, you practice lunging against a wall until your tongue's hanging out. That ought to take the kinks out of your quadriceps femoris."

He went out, leaving me alone in the examining room behind Stern's office. I'd been told to wait for the top man himself, and if I knew my medical bureaucrats, it was going to be a long wait. They've got to put us field men in our places, even if we do get to call them by their first names.

I took my time pulling on my pants therefore, and I could have taken more. After I'd waited fifteen minutes, a prim young woman came in and told me Dr. Stern had been taken suddenly busy and wouldn't be able to see me this morning. He was terribly sorry, she said. I said I shared his grief; and I went over to the gym and made arrangements with Martinelli, the edged-weapons trainer.

He was very glad to have someone to fence with. The current crop of recruits had apparently all been taught never to lead with their rights. It was almost impossible, the Dago said, to make a good fencer or knifeman of a kid brought up to fight left foot forward, in the American boxing tradition. Such a candidate did everything backwards as far as real, permanent mayhem was concerned. All he was good for was punching people in the nose with his lousy straight left.

I listened to Martinelli's plaints for a while, knowing that I was stalling. I was trying to make up my mind about something; I was telling myself not to be sentimental and mix into stuff that was none of my business. When I figured I had myself convinced, I got the map coordinates of the nearest security booth, navigated my way there, and called Washington on the direct phone.

I had a little trouble getting hold of Mac, which was unusual. There's a theory to the effect that he's actually a limited-production robot, several identical copies of which have been installed in several identical offices, each with a bright window facing you so you can't see too clearly what you're talking to. Extras are switched on as needed to handle the flow of traffic. You never know which Mac-machine you're getting, but it doesn't matter, since they're all tuned to the same wave length and function off the same master computer, down in the basement somewhere. Personally, I don't believe a word of it. They haven't got computers that sarcastic yet.

When I did get him, he said, "Congratulations, Eric. Or should we change the code name to Casanova."

I sighed. "Dr. Tommy's been on the phone, I suppose. That's why he didn't want to face me this morning. He's been making complaints behind my back."

"He was just on the line. He tells me that even sick and psychotic young ladies find you so irresistible they leave their hospital beds and break the self-imposed silence of weeks rather than be parted from you. Dr. Stern is disturbed. The gist of his lengthy discourse was that he feels that you have, in a sense, been practicing medicine without a license—all wrong. He reminds me that Sheila was assigned to you only for transportation, not for brutal amateur therapy."

"Brutal?" I said. "Hell, I haven't touched the girl. Except for last night when I didn't know who or what she was. Nothing personal was intended, I assure you."

"I gather that the brutality to which Dr. Stern objects was mental rather than physical. He says that you deliberately poked fun at her appearance with a cruel nickname, even in his presence, and jibed at her for being poor company. He feels that you are probably responsible for giving her a strong feeling of guilt about her conduct in Costa Verde, a feeling that will complicate her cure tremendously. He claims that the patient has responded masochistically to this crude treatment of yours—transference is the word he used, I believe—and that the dependency-relationship thus established, if continued, will make it quite impossible for him to communicate with her and guide her recovery, in any constructive way. I hope I have all the terms correct. Dr. Stern requests, therefore, that you be ordered to leave the patient strictly alone from now on." Mac paused and went on: "Is there any reason why I should not give such an order, Eric?"

It was my turn to hesitate. I reminded myself again not to be a sentimental slob. "No, sir," I said.

"Very well. So much for that. You'll be interested to know that President Avila of Costa Verde has carried out a thorough investigation of the matter submitted to him by the government of the United States. He is happy to report that there is no basis whatever for the rumor that the so-called revolutionary forces had a nuclear missile in their possession. No traces of such a missile have been found. President Avila is glad to have been of service, and hopes we will give him more opportunities to prove his friendship and spirit of cooperation. End of message."

"Rumor, hell!" I said. I made a face at the wall of the booth. "So it's like that, eh?"

"Just like that. I won't risk your hanging up by asking if you actually saw a Rudovic III in that jungle clearing."

I said, "Well, no, I'll tell you, sir. I got the description

from an article in the Sunday papers. I thought it would
liven things up in Washington, kind of."

"Yes, to be sure," Mac said. "Well, we'll let the diplo-
mats worry about it. Have you studied your instructions?"

"Yes, sir."

"You will start your interviewing program in Tucson a
week from Wednesday, to synchronize with a legitimate survey being conducted in other cities. You have eleven blocks
to cover. In each of those eleven blocks, you will interview one person in each household as an authorized interviewer for an organization known as Market Research
Associates, Inc."

"Yes, sir. I got that out of the instruction booklet. I
was hoping I hadn't. You did say *every* household in
eleven blocks?"

"That is correct. That is the technique used by the company by which you are ostensibly employed. In each of the
selected blocks, there is only one address that is of real
interest to us, but if the people at that address become
suspicious, we hope it will reassure them to learn that every-
one else in the block has also been visited by the MRA
interviewer. I can't tell you exactly what to look for. We
are trying to find a pattern, something these eleven homes,
or at least one person in each of them, have in common."

"Yes, sir," I said. "You mean like two arms, two legs,
and a head, sir?"

"More like Heinrich von Sachs," he said. "These addresses
were visited in a systematic way by a man known to have
been associated with von Sachs, a man who was spotted
entering the U.S. from Mexico at a small border town in
Arizona called Antelope Wells, somewhere east of Nogales,
according to my information."

I said, "It's east, all right. It's over the state line in
New Mexico."

"Indeed? I should have checked the map. You know the
town, Eric?"

"Now you're exaggerating, sir. It's hardly a town, it's
just a gate in the international fence. They used to close
it at night and on weekends, as I recall. Maybe they still
do. On our side, there's a little shack for the customs and
immigration man. On the other side there are half a dozen
adobe houses, a handful of trees, and a few Mexican
border officials. South of that there's nothing for ninety
miles except a couple of ruts across the desert, and I mean

desert. It's one of the most Godforsaken hunks of real estate on earth, just rocks, sand, cactus, and mesquite, with a bunch of desolate mountains peeking over the horizon after you get down a ways—called the Nacimientos, I think."

Mac said, "It has been determined that a permit was issued to von Sachs under another name to do some archaeological work in the Nacimiento Mountains. The question is where. As you say, it's a wild area; it is also a large one. The department working on the job before it was transferred to us reports that efforts to trace him from the Mexican end have proved fruitless. I think our first step should be to determine if one of these people in Tucson has the information."

"What about the man who visited them, von Sachs' associate, so-called. He must know where he came from, when he appeared at Antelope Wells."

"If he knows, he isn't saying. Unfortunately the gentleman must be referred to in the past tense."

"I see," I said. "That helps. That's just ducky. What happened?"

"He was trailed to Tucson. Apparently he was some kind of a courier or contact man. Note was made of the addresses he visited. He started for Phoenix; apparently he had several cities on his route. However, something frightened him and he turned back hurriedly, heading towards Antelope Wells. Somebody decided he should be picked up for questioning before he disappeared below the border, but the arresting officers were careless, and he got his hand to his mouth. It is recorded that he cried 'Viva Quintana' and gave a smart salute before falling on his face, dead of cyanide. The salute he gave was the old straight-armed Nazi salute."

I said wryly, "It sounds just like Old Home Week. Who's Quintana?"

"Who but friend Heinrich? In Mexico he is Kurt Quintana, son of a German mother and a Mexican father. The documents proving this are fraudulent, of course, but until it's established, he is a citizen. He can have you arrested if you bother him."

"I'll keep it in mind."

"I understand your station wagon is ailing mechanically. There is a reasonably new Volkswagen in Phoenix you can have if you like. As for weapons," Mac went on, "if you need anything special, you'll have to supply yourself locally or give us time to send out what you want. If you need an assistant, one can be provided. There are some young people at the ranch for training, one of whom might as well be picking up a little practical experience. He could, for instance, get the interviews started while you make a preliminary investigation along the border."

"Well, eleven blocks is a lot of houses," I said. "I wouldn't mind a little help, but I don't particularly want a green kid tagging along." I hesitated. The idea that had come into my mind was ridiculous, but I heard myself saying: "What about Sheila? She's been around long enough to learn the ropes a little."

"Sheila?" It took a lot to surprise him, but I'd managed.

"She wants out," I said. "Out of here. That's what she came to tell me last night."

"It's out of the question," Mac said. "Dr. Stern says—"

"Dr. Tommy has a thing about curing people, I'm afraid," I said. "I think he sometimes forgets that his job isn't to make us into perfectly adjusted human beings, it's to return us to the front lines in good shooting condition. Hell, if he ever managed to adjust us, we'd quit this racket. The girl walks and talks now, and she wants out."

"You're being sentimental," Mac said.

"Yes, sir."

"She is in no shape to—"

"To ask silly questions and record the silly answers on a questionnaire? If she isn't now, she will be in ten days. It could be a damn sight better for her than staying here and having Tommy and his nurses tinkering with her subconscious. Occupational therapy, we call it."

There was a long silence. Then his voice came reluctantly: "You'd be responsible, Eric. And remember, we have doctors on the payroll but you're not one of them. You have other duties, which must come first."

"Yes, sir."

"There is no accounting for tastes, of course," he said deliberately. "But I thought there was a lady in Texas—"

I said, "What's my love life got to do with this?"

"Then what—"

I grimaced at the sound-proof paneling in front of me. "As you say, I'm being sentimental, sir. Do you remember a man we called Vance?"

"Why, yes. He died up in northern Europe."

"Yes, sir. And do you remember a man we called Le-Baron?"

"Yes. He died. . . . Oh, I begin to see. Vaguely."

"Yes, sir. LeBaron was killed in Juarez, Mexico, helping me. Vance was killed in Kiruna, Sweden, helping me. And how many other good agents have I taken out and lost in the line of duty? So when for once in my life I find one instead and bring her back alive, I'd just kind of like to see that she makes it all the way. Dr. Tommy himself will admit he can't do anything for her unless she wants him to, and she doesn't. Maybe I can."

"Very well." His voice was crisp. "As I say, it's your responsibility. She can start the interviews a week from Wednesday. You'd better head down towards Antelope Wells as soon as the medical department approves. But be sure you get back to Tucson in time to take over if something goes wrong."

I said, "Yes, sir. If she blows up on the job I'll ship the pieces back here and handle the rest of it myself."

"Just remember," he said, "the mental health of one agent, or even her life, or yours, is not really significant against the larger picture."

He was starting to talk like an ad man in his old age. "The larger picture," I said. "Yes, sir. We'll get you von Sachs."

VIII

THE BORDER COUNTRY hadn't changed much in the time I'd been away. It was still a barren, yellowish-gray-green landscape with only an occasional cottonwood for a tree and an occasional dark mountain range to break the monotony of the rolling, empty plain. The farther south I proceeded towards Antelope Wells, the less there was to see. Anybody who wants to call it a desert will get no argument from me, although once in a while I'd drive past a windmill and water tank that would seem to indicate that this desolate-looking land was, after all, owned by somebody and used for raising something besides cactus and rattlesnakes.

After asking all the questions I could think of down there—finding somebody to ask was the real problem—I headed back to Tucson where I stopped in a sporting goods store that had a selection of hunting rifles, some with real pretty stocks dolled up with decorative inlays and thick rubber recoil pads. Unfortunately I was spending the government's money, and I doubted that I could prove to a cold-eyed department accountant that a fancy gun shoots better than a plain one, since I didn't really believe it myself. As for recoil pads, there's a theory to the effect that a lot of soft rubber between you and the gun just gives it a running start before it socks you.

Acting like a deer hunter getting a jump on the season, I picked out a standard light Winchester M70, therefore, in the good old reliable .30-06 caliber. They had some Magnums on the rack, but I didn't have the time or the facilities to fix up this gun like the one I'd left with Jiminez in Costa Verde. I'd have to shoot standard factory ammunition, for one thing, instead of working out a special load for the gun.

It couldn't be an extra-long-range, super-precision deal this time, and the lighter cartridge would shoot far enough for the accuracy I could expect, besides being easier on the shoulder. I bought several boxes in each of several bullet weights. You never know which bullet a gun is going to like best until you try it. I got a medium-priced four-power scope and had them mount it while I waited.

Then I took my packages out to the car, which was still the old Pontiac station wagon, partially rejuvenated under the hood. With two of us on the job, two cars had been needed, and this seemed to be one of those years when CIA or somebody had got to all the undercover dough first. Since I was in better condition to deal with mechanical emergencies than Sheila, I was driving the antique.

I hadn't seen her since the previous weekend. We'd met for a final briefing session under the cold eye of Dr. Tom Stern, who'd done his best to discourage the whole idea, but she hadn't let him scare her. I looked for the Volkswagen now as I drove up to the modest tourist court that had been selected as our headquarters in Tucson. I'd been told the car was blue, but there were no four-wheeled foreign bugs of any color around. Well, it was still relatively early in the afternoon, and she should be out interviewing. Nevertheless I found myself disappointed and a little worried. I hoped she hadn't had a relapse or anything. *It's your responsibility*, Mac had said.

She'd made a reservation for me around the corner from her unit—also around the corner from the pool, which was full of yelling kids. In that part of the country, even the crummiest hostelries have pools these days. Coronado wouldn't know the place. I moved my stuff inside, made a routine check around the room, and lay down on the big double bed after making sure the air conditioner was working full blast. There wouldn't be anything new to think about until I'd talked with my assistant. In the business, you learn to grab sleep when you can, so I did.

I was awakened, presently, by a knocking on the door: three short raps followed after a pause by two more. Under certain circumstances this tells the person behind the door that it isn't necessary to go for the firearms or depart by the window; under other circumstances, such as the present, it just means *hello, it's me*. I got up, yawned, and went over to let her in.

"Mr. Evans?" she said for the benefit of anyone who might be listening. "Mr. Evans, I'm Sheila Summerton. I'm sorry I wasn't here when you arrived. I was conducting some interviews on the other side of town, and I didn't think you'd get in so early."

"It's perfectly all right," I said. "I'm sorry you had to start on the job alone, but I simply couldn't break away sooner. Won't you come in?"

I stepped back to let her pass. It was the first time, I realized, that I'd seen her in a dress, a thin, sleeveless, full-skirted number in a gay summer print that somehow managed to make her look very small and fragile. I was a little startled to realize that I was as glad to see her as if she were somebody I knew and liked, instead of just a responsibility I'd taken on for some screwy reason of sentiment.

I closed the door. "Hi, Skinny," I said.

She frowned quickly, and glanced around the room. "Should we. . . . I mean, is it safe to talk?"

"I've made a rough check. Do you have any reason to believe anybody's interested enough in us to bug our rooms?"

She shook her head. "No. It's been very dull. And very hot."

"How far have you got?"

"Two blocks completed. One almost finished. I should clean that up tonight or tomorrow morning."

I said, "You weren't supposed to kill yourself, Skinny. Your instructions were to take it easy. Three blocks in three days is overdoing it. You look like hell."

"Thanks," she murmured. "There's nothing like appreciation and flattery to make the troops feel good." Then she began to cry. She just stood there, holding a brief case in the hand that had the tips of the fingers individually bandaged now, looking at me with the tears running down her face. "Oh, d-damn it," she breathed. "I'm sorry. I guess I am a little t-tired."

"Sure," I said. I reached out and took the briefcase and set it aside. "Sit down before you fall down."

She didn't move at once. I put my arm about her shoulders to lead her to a chair, and everything kind of stopped in the room, if you know what I mean. She went perfectly still. After a moment she looked slowly from my face to the hand on her shoulder. The funny yellow light was in her eyes.

"Excuse me," I said, taking my hand away.

She went to the bed and sat down. After a moment she looked up and said in a perfectly normal voice, "I'm sorry. Thats silly; I'll have to get over it. You don't happen to have a spare hanky?"

I got her a clean one out of the dresser drawer. While she was mopping up, I took the cardboard ice bucket provided by the management and went out to fill it at the machine near the office. When I returned, she was sitting where I'd left her, but her face was dry and she had the brief case at her feet, open.

"I'm sorry I made a scene," she said. "It's been pretty hot and my feet hurt. Do you want to hear my report?"

"If you want to give it," I said. "No rush."

"I've got two of the key interviews so far—the addresses that were visited by von Sachs' courier or recruiter or whatever he was. The first place, 2032 Montezuma Avenue. Fred Winter. A cheap little house in a trashy suburb. The payments are made by Mrs. Winter, a schoolteacher. Winter, a mechanic when he's working, seems to spend most of his time in front of the television drinking beer by the gallon —judging by the empties—and complaining about his back and other things. Radio, TV. No phonograph or tape re-corder. No short-wave equipment in evidence."

I put a drink into her hand. "Go on, I'm listening."

"Address number two, 174½ Rosario Lane. Eladio Griego. It's an adobe shack in Spanish-town, or whatever they call it here. The mother can hardly speak English. I interviewed her, since Eladio's been in jail since last week for knifing a man. It's happened before, I gather."

"But he wasn't in jail at the time the courier came around?"

"No. They've got a radio but it doesn't work. There's a functioning TV. No phonograph or tape recorder. The place was dark and full of broken-down furniture. There could have been all kinds of electronic equipment hidden in the mess, but I don't really think there was."

I frowned. "Of course, we don't know that it's the man of the house who's involved in every case. Come to that, we don't even know that every address that was visited is significant. The guy could have taken time off to call on his girl, or his favorite uncle, or something."

"Well, so far I'd say we have two good prospects," Sheila said. "I didn't meet Mrs. Winter, she was busy at school. But her husband is a surly brute with a grudge against society, which makes him a promising candidate. Old Mrs. Griego is feeble and half blind, but her Eladio is apparently a husky boy who'd kick your head in just for fun. Good strong-arm material."

"Unfortunately Eladio's not going to do us much good in jail," I said. "We'd have to pull too many strings to get at him. We have to find somebody we can work on easily, who knows where von Sachs-Quintana has his head-quarters down in Mexico. This beer-swilling Winter char-acter doesn't sound as if he'd be trusted with that kind of information, even if he is a member of the outfit." I sipped my drink. "Anything promising in this third block you've been working?"

Sheila glanced down at a paper in her hand. "Number three," she said, "1420 Mimosa Street. Ernest Head. He seems to be a little better off than the first two, judging by the house. He was in when I called, but he'd just got home from work and his wife said he was tired and asked me to come back after dinner. I—" She stopped, frowning.

"What is it?"

"There was something funny. I've just remembered. I wanted to ask you about it."

"Go on and ask."

"I'm trying to think of it. There was a record player going in a house kind of catty-corner across the back yard. It was turned very loud and the window was open. One of the numbers that was played . . . it made me feel funny. I mean, it had associations. I'd heard it before, somewhere. I have a feeling it's important."

"Why?"

"I don't know. It just seemed terribly out of place, somehow. Dum dum dum dum, ta dum ta dum ta dum ta. . . . Do you recognize it?"

I grinned. "Well, not really."

"Oh, dear," she said ruefully. "I never could carry a tune. I wish I could remember where I'd heard it before."

"Did you check the house?"

"Of course."

"It isn't one of our key addresses?"

"No. I told you. I was going up to that when I heard this music from another place behind it." Sheila hesitated. "If you'd drive out there tonight with me, you could wait outside and listen. Maybe she'll play it again. I have a feeling you'd recognize it."

"She?"

"Apparently it's a woman. Miss Catherine Smith, it said on the mailbox."

I regarded her for a moment. "You really think this is worth my sitting in the car a couple of hours, Skinny?"

She moved her small shoulders briefly. "Call it a hunch," she said. "I know it sounds silly, but—"

"You win," I said. "I didn't survive in this business by passing up anybody's hunches. But if it turns out to be Elvis Presley who makes you feel funny, you'll buy me a drink."

IX

IT WAS QUITE a concert. Miss Smith, if that was her name, had a lot of records, and her equipment had lots of volume. Even at the distance I was parked, I had no trouble identifying her selections. Her closer neighbors must have been either very tolerant or very deaf, to put up with the racket. But then, in a development like that, I guess you have to learn to live with each other's taste in music.

It was a machine-made oasis at the edge of Tucson, fairly new—parts were still being built up—known as Saguaro Heights. It had reasonable-sized cinder-block houses in pink, blue, yellow, and green. Each house had a TV antenna on the roof and a little lawn out front. The farther out into the desert some people move, the stronger seems to be this compulsion they get to grow and mow grass.

I was sitting in the station wagon across the street from the residence of Mr. and Mrs. Ernest Head. The Heads had a small ornate evergreen tree and some gaudy semi-tropical flowers. Judging by a tricycle and other debris, they also had kids. A shiny new car, one of the new compact Pontiacs—a far cry from my massive relic—was parked on the short concrete apron that connected the garage with the street.

There was a space of about twenty feet between the Head house, blue, and the pink house next door. Looking through this gap I could see, diagonally across back yards full of swings and clotheslines, the open window from which the music seemed to be coming. Nothing had shown at it yet.

I glanced at my watch and yawned. Well, it was one of our significant interviews and Sheila was right to spend as much time as she decently could inside. Maybe she was learning something. However, the night was hot and the station wagon upholstery was lumpy with age. I yawned again, trying to find stretching room for my legs. The door across the street opened, and Sheila came out. She looked pretty and unfamiliar in her summer dress and high heels.

There were only the white-bandaged tips of her fingers to remind me of the tattered scrap of female humanity I'd helped haul out of the Costa Verde jungle. She crossed the street and came to my window.

"Well?" she asked eagerly.

"No picture but lots of sound," I said. "Selections from 'My Fair Lady'. Part of the Swan Lake Ballet Suite. Some waltzes, Strauss, and I think a bit of Lehar. She keeps getting tired of a piece and switching to something else. Currently, as you can hear, Siegfried is having a rough time getting to the Rhine. He may make it and then again he may not."

"Oh," Sheila said, disappointed. "I'm sorry. I guess I got you here for nothing."

"No strain," I said. "It's been a great cultural experience. Did you spot anything inside?"

She shook her head. "There was nothing out of line that I could see. Mr. Head sells cars. His wife is nice, a handsome dark woman, and the two kids are cute. There's a phonograph for the kids, and a TV of course, and there are three radios: a clock-radio in the bedroom, a little set in the kitchen for Mrs. H, and an expensive all-wave portable they bought recently to take along when they go camping. Mrs. H says she's listened to the BBC on it."

"That could mean something," I said. "A long-range receiver like that."

"Maybe. There was no hint of any sending equipment or other short-wave stuff." Sheila looked up, listening. "What's our music-mad lady playing now?"

"She's starting to pick them loud and brassy for a woman," I said. "From Wagner to Sousa. 'King Cotton March.' Does it make you feel funny? Does it have associations?"

She shook her head. "Well, I guess that's all for tonight. I'll come back and clean up this block in the morning."

"Sure."

She started around the car, hesitated, and looked back. "Thanks," she said.

"For what?"

"For being nice about it. For not telling me I'm a silly fool, hearing things."

I regarded her for a moment, and told myself firmly I didn't really like thin little girls with big eyes that changed color disconcertingly.

"Come on, get in," I said. "Don't make me sit on these lopsided springs any longer than—"

I stopped. The distant music had changed again, and there it was, clear and unbelievable. It was a hell of a thing to hear on a starry night in a peaceful residential development in Tucson, Arizona. It took me back to another continent and another time. I was aware that Sheila had started to speak and stopped, realizing from my expression, I guess, that she didn't have to say anything.

After a moment I cleared my throat and looked at her. "For God's sake, Skinny. You mean you didn't recognize *that?*"

She licked her lips. "I still don't. Maybe it was played for us in training, but my memory for music is terrible. What—"

"Hold it," I said softly. "Easy does it. Laugh as if I'd said something funny."

I heard her laugh. I was looking past her, across the street. Strains of the music were still drifting across the back yards from the open, empty, lighted window. Nearer, a man was stumbling around the side of the Heads' garage towards us.

"Laugh and talk," I said. "Then look around casually. Is that Ernest Head?"

Sheila laughed again. "Oh, Mr. Evans, that's priceless!" she giggled, leaning against the car in a casual way that let her look across the street. Her voice reached me softly. "Yes, that's Head. Did you see his *face?*"

"I saw it," I said. "He's hearing music from the grave, I think. I am now telling a dirty joke about. . . . Well, you name it. He's heading for his car. Be ready to get in. We're going to make like detectives if he drives off."

Head stopped by his new little Pontiac, a stocky, balding man in shirtsleeves. As he opened the car door, the courtesy light went on inside and showed me his face clearly. It was the face of a man who'd seen death, or heard it.

"But what is it?" Sheila whispered. "What is the piece?"

"I guess it was just a little before your time," I said. "And lots of people talked about it, but relatively few really knew it, in this country, at least. What you're hearing is an orchestral version of a ditty called the Horst Wessel Song. Somebody is being clever, I think, not to say mildly fiendish."

Across the street, Mr. Ernest Head, car salesman, backed

his shiny new car away from his neat new house and drove
away as if devils were after him, and I guess they were.
I could hear them in the music, too, but they weren't my
devils. Not now. They'd given me a hard time once—me
and a few million other men—but now after nearly twenty
years they were just some half-forgotten clowns in brown
uniforms and heavy boots who'd had a catchy song and a
funny way of marching. They'd presented a problem, sure,
but we'd solved it the hard way. Or had we?

"Get in, Skinny," I said. "Here we go."

Driving away, I watched the rear-view mirror carefully.
I studied the evening traffic around us. Tucson is a typical,
sprawling southwestern city, with wide streets that make
an inconspicuous tailing job relatively easy. The only trouble
was, this would work two ways. Presently I turned off,
letting the little Pontiac keep on going. Sheila glanced at
me quickly.

"You're letting him go?"

"No sense having him spot us following," I said. "He
saw the car parked by his house. I have a hunch he's just
driving around to settle his nerves where his family can't
see him, anyway."

"Then why—"

"I wanted to see if anyone else was interested in where
he was heading. Nobody seems to be. Whoever's playing
that tune, call her Miss Smith, either she's got no outside
help to watch Head while she tends the turntable, or she's
got reason to think he's going nowhere important, at least
tonight." I grimaced. "Maybe it's a break. The question is
how to use it. Let's get back to the motel and do some
thinking."

Nobody followed us. I made sure of this. There were
still kids around the pool when I drove past it and parked
the station wagon in the slot in front of my unit, around
the corner.

"I'd ask you in for a drink, Miss Summerton," I said
rather loudly, "if I could be sure my motives wouldn't be
misconstrued."

She laughed. "Don't be silly, Mr. Evans. This isn't the
reign of Queen Victoria, you know. Besides, we'd better
decide how we're going to split the work tomorrow."

"Well, in that case—"

I unlocked and opened the door, switched on the light,
waited for her to enter, and closed the door behind her.

"I think we're overdoing the Miss Summerton-Mr. Evans routine," she said after a moment. "We'd better get to be Sheila and Hank tomorrow, don't you think?"

I gave her a grin. "And honey and darling the next day?" It was just something I threw out without thinking. Like my hand on her shoulder, it made her freeze up instantly. Her face got cold and remote and a little pale. I said quickly, "It's a good suggestion. Maybe I was hamming it up a bit. But now let's hear your thoughts about a disc jockey named Smith."

She didn't seem to hear me. She had turned away from me, perhaps so I wouldn't be able to see her face. I couldn't guess what she was thinking, except that it probably wasn't pleasant, or flattering to me. Well, I'd been clumsy again. On the other hand, as she'd said herself, she was going to have to get over it some day.

She caught sight of the long cardboard box marked Winchester that I'd left lying on the bed, on the theory that hiding eight pounds and three feet of high-powered rifle in a small motel room isn't really feasible and merely calls attention to what you're trying to conceal. In that part of the U.S. people tend to take hunting rifles for granted, anyway. Sheila stepped forward, opened the box, and looked at the weapon inside. After a moment she turned to look at me accusingly, as if she thought I'd been keeping things from her.

"Just an item that may come in handy," I said. "I picked it up on my way through town this afternoon."

"But you must have found a lead of some kind down along the border or you wouldn't have—"

I shook my head. "No such luck. It's just that kind of wide-open country, clear down into Mexico. Even when we get von Sachs' mountain hideout located, we may not be able to work in very close."

I watched her lift the gun out of the box and, like any well-trained marksman, slip the bolt back to make certain the piece was unloaded. It gave me a funny feeling to watch her and remember that this small, frail-looking person had gone to a very tough school and learned, among other things, how to handle a large number of lethal weapons, many of which the average man had never seen or heard of.

"Careful," I said. "You'll get your dress dirty. It's right off the rack; it's still got the factory preservative."

She laid it back in the box and rubbed her hands together. "You haven't fired it yet?"

"No," I said. "We'll have to sneak off tomorrow and find a place where we can sight it in."

She gave me a sharp glance. "We?"

"I want you to have the feel of it, too. We don't know how this will break." I looked at her. "Unless, of course, you have some objection."

"No," she said quickly. "No, of course not." After a moment she said, "Then you didn't have much luck on your border trip?"

"Well, I didn't really expect to pick up any information on von Sachs. That's what we're here in Tucson for. I did get some road information from some anthropologists digging up old pots on one of the ranches down there. They were down the road past the Nacimientos, well down into Mexico, earlier this summer. Apparently it's no place to go for a Sunday drive. They used jeeps. An ordinary car might make it, they said, but it would be a real rough trip. Anyway, I learned enough from them that I figure once we get some kind of a lead to von Sachs' mountain hideout, I can probably find my way there."

"But they hadn't seen him?"

"They hadn't actually been up in the rocks. They didn't seem to think there was anything back there except lizards and gophers and a few caves that might have been inhabited by humans a thousand years ago but weren't now. Apparently it's great country for caves." I glanced at my watch. "Well, I think I'll head back to Saguaro Heights and tackle the musical Miss Smith."

Sheila frowned. "Do you think that's wise?"

"I can't see any reason not to stick to our market-research cover just because some gal plays a few records," I said. "You'd better take the body around the corner and put it to bed. See you in the morning."

X

MISS SMITH'S HOUSE was green, even newer than the one in front of which I'd waited for Sheila, earlier. The lawn wasn't fully established yet. The tree in front was a small, new weeping willow, the pale yellow-green variety that's considered to have more class—in landscaping and gardening circles—than the old-fashioned dark green. There were no tricycles or roller skates.

By the time I got back there, the concert was over for the evening, or at least for the time being. I had to ring twice before anything happened inside. Then footsteps approached the front door. There was that funny little moment that comes when you reach what may be the turning point of a job, when you don't know whether a door is just going to open or the world is going to blow up in your face. The lighting fixture above the front steps came on. A chain was unhooked, a lock was unlocked, the door swung back, and there she was.

It was quite a production. There was a good deal of fine, artificial-looking, pinky-blonde hair fluffed and pinned about her head in an elaborate fashion. It looked like the nylon hair they put on dolls these days. There were baby-blue eyes with long black lashes and lots of surrounding make-up, the kind that looks as if it ought to glow in the dark. There was a big, soft, promising red mouth, and there was a figure constructed to back up the promise, more or less veiled by a short black negligee, like a ruffly, semi-transparent, knee-length coat.

What was worn under the negligee, although partially obscured, seemed to be black also, short on coverage and long on interest. There was a pair of very handsome legs in smoky stockings, and there was a pair of high-heeled, bedroom-type slippers or mules without much to hold them on except the little black rosettes at the toes. It was fairly obvious that Miss Smith had expected her musical invitation to be accepted by someone, and had dressed accordingly.

"Ye-es?" she said in a husky voice.

"I'm sorry to bother you ma'am," I said humbly. "My name is Evans, ma'am. I work for a company called Market Research Associates. We're doing a survey in this area, and I wondered if you'd be kind enough to let me ask you a few questions—"

"A survey?" Her attitude was impatient. "What kind of a survey?"

"We're studying people's buying habits, ma'am," I said, "with particular reference to television sets, radios, phonographs, and tape recorders. It's kind of impertinent, I guess, but I'm supposed to find out what you own in this line, when you bought it, where you keep it, and how often you use it."

She studied my face for a moment. The blue eyes with the mascara-blackened lashes were surprisingly keen. She was by no means the dumb sexpot she was pretending to be. I knew what she was thinking. I wasn't the person she'd expected. I might even be a perfectly innocent interviewer for a perfectly respectable research outfit, an irrelevant nuisance. And then again, I might not be.

"Well, all right," she said reluctantly. "Come in, Mr. Evans. I hope this isn't going to take too long. It's getting pretty late."

"I'll make it as snappy as I can, ma'am," I said. "I certainly appreciate—"

"Never mind that. Just come in and ask your damn questions."

"Yes, ma'am."

Inside, there was wall-to-wall carpeting and mass-production furniture of more or less modern design. There were some crates and boxes shoved away in corners, and traces of excelsior to indicate recent unpacking. A medium-priced stereo record player held court at the front of the living room with both speakers aimed towards the window in the dining area at the rear that was essentially part of the same room. Beside the machine was a shelf of records. Several empty cardboard sleeves lay on top, presumably belonging to the records currently on the spindle.

Miss Smith closed the front door and came over to switch on a light by the sofa. She indicated the low, glass-topped cocktail table.

"You can spread your stuff there. Just what did you want to know?" She watched me sit down, open my brief case, and take out a questionnaire form before answering. "My God," she said, "if we're going to collaborate on a damn book, I need a drink. What about you?"

I was still busily organizing my materials and listening to her voice. She was good, very good, but she'd picked too difficult a part to play. She was working hard to sound like a crude and obvious American person, but there was a hint of an accent that gave her away. The hardest thing in the world is to swear convincingly in a language that isn't your own.

"What did you say, ma'am?" I asked.

"Do you want a drink?"

"Oh, no, ma'am." I was laying it on thick, also, but then I wanted her to know I was playing a part. It would be interesting to see who she thought I was, if I wasn't Henry Evans, interviewer. "No, thank you, ma'am. Now, this is 103 Maple Drive, isn't it? And the mailbox says your name is Smith, Catherine Smith. Is that right?"

She'd moved over to the corner to pour herself a drink at a little cabinet that apparently served as a bar.

"That's right. You have sharp eyes, Mr. Evans."

"Oh, we learn to notice things like that," I said smugly. "Now, are you the female head of the household, Miss Smith?"

She laughed. "Well, I'm female, I pay the bills, and it's my house. I just bought it. As you can see, we're not all moved in yet."

"Then you don't live here alone?"

"No, my father's living with me. Papa's retired, and he hasn't been well since Mama died. . . . What are you doing now?"

She'd come to stand over me disturbingly. There was a high concentration of some heavy perfume. Fortunately, I've never been particularly susceptible to smells; I react better to visual stimuli. However, she was being quite generous with those, too.

I cleared my throat and said, "Well, it's a statistical thing, Miss Smith. I fill in your name in this little box, so. Then I fill in your dad's name—"

"Herman Smith," she said when I paused. "It used to be Schmidt, a good Kraut name, but Papa had it changed."

I wrote it down. "Herman Smith. Now some statistician back at the company has put an X in the box of this particular questionnaire opposite the person I should inter- view here if the household contains two people. Every questionnaire is pre-marked that way. That's so I don't talk to only the pretty girls in the homes I visit."

I looked up and grinned boldly. She smiled back, but her eyes remained sharp and searching.

"You mean they don't trust you, Mr. Evans?" Her voice was light. "Why, you look terribly trustworthy to me! I'd never have let you into my house at this hour if you didn't."

I cleared my throat again. "Well, they have lots of inter- viewers. Let's say they don't trust all of them to be, er, completely objective. The head office wants to be sure of getting a random sampling in every block we survey."

"You're doing this whole block, then?"

"Yes, ma'am. That is, my assistant and I are doing it. She's been around here all day. Maybe you saw her, a girl in a blue Volkswagen. She was kind of tired tonight, so I said I'd finish up."

The blue eyes were puzzled. Now I had an assistant; I was interviewing a whole block, not just Catherine Smith. It was a big deal. I had a raft of questionnaires, all looking very authentic. I had a dumb look and a corny line of patter. Maybe I really was just an innocent doorbell-ringer after all.

I glanced down at the form on the table. I looked up and met her eyes deliberately. "In this case, Miss Smith, it just happens to work out that I'm supposed to interview the female head of the house."

She got the message. She murmured, "That's lucky for you, since Papa happens to be out at the movies."

Her voice was dry. She was smiling faintly. She knew me now. At least she knew, because I'd just told her, that if my questionnaire hadn't specified the female head of the household, I would have rigged it so it did—and as a matter of fact, I had. I answered her smile with a significant look she was free to interpret as she pleased. I was gambling for a real reaction, and I got it.

She walked over to the record player and paused to look back at me dubiously. She was still not quite sure. Then she moved her shoulders in a reckless sort of shrug and bent over the machine. There was some clattering and scratching before she found the right band on the right record, followed by a few bars of music that could have led to anything. Suddenly the Horst Wessel Lied was filling the room, seeming to come from all around us.

I've never been much of a stereo man. The idea of hearing a record poorly reproduced from two directions instead of one doesn't seem like a real acoustical breakthrough to me. In this case, however, perhaps because the volume was turned very high, perhaps because the music had strong associations for me, the effect was almost hypnotic. I could practically hear again the heavy boots striking the pavement in that ridiculous goosestep that hadn't been a bit funny at the time.

I got up slowly. Catherine Smith was standing by the

player watching me. She was a good-looking woman dressed for love, if you want to call it that, but for a moment it meant nothing to me and, I saw, nothing to her, either. The slightly parted lips, the bright eyes, with which she listened to the song that once shook the world, were signs of a different kind of passion.

She'd made her move. It was my turn now. I faced her, waiting while the instruments worked their way through some fancy orchestration and hit the tune again.

"Die Fahne hoch," I said, speaking the words in time to the music, *"die Reihen fest geschlossen, SA marchiert mit ruhig festen schritt. . . ."* My accent wasn't half bad, I thought. I looked into the woman's eyes and went on, deadpan: "That's German, Miss Smith. It means, 'With banners high and closed ranks, SA marches with calm and steady stride.' SA stands for *Sturmabteilung.* In English, you know, they were commonly known as Storm Troopers."

Her eyes never left my face. We'd reached some more stuff with drums and brasses. She waited. The theme came through, clear and disturbing. At least I'd known it well enough, once, to be disturbed by it. It was like having a snake come back to life after you'd chopped off its head.

Catherine Smith hummed softly along with the music. She let the first bars go by. Her accurate contralto picked up the tune and the closing words: ". . . . *es schaut auf Haakenkreuz vol Hoffnung schon Millionen. Der Tag fur Freiheit und fur Brot bricht an!"*

The song came to an abrupt end. She reached out and switched off the record player without looking that way. Her eyes were very blue and bright, watching me steadily.

"The *Haakenkreuz* is the swastika, you know." Her voice was soft.

"I know," I said. I hoped I was making the right responses.

It was very quiet in the room with the record player still. "Freedom and bread!" she murmured. "It has been a long time since those great days, Henry Evans. A long time. But perhaps they will come again!"

XI

To BE HONEST, it wasn't exactly what I'd expected. When I'd first heard that music, and seen Ernest Head's panicky reaction to it, I'd assumed it was meant as a threat, a promise of vengeance perhaps, a warning of retribution to come. Certainly he'd seemed to be taking it that way.

I'd jumped to certain conclusions about Head's past—after all, Head translates to *kopf* in German, and there are a lot of good Teutonic names ending with that syllable. I'd even done some fancy guessing about Catherine Smith's motives in broadcasting sweet Nazi sounds to drive him crazy. I hadn't really expected to find that she was a Heil-Hitler girl herself. Well, it's always a mistake to theorize on insufficient data. I'd followed her lead, and this was where we'd got.

I walked over to the shelf and picked up one of the empty record sleeves. It looked authentic enough, decorated with a slick photo montage of marching soldiers in various uniforms, but the recording company was one I'd never heard of. The title was "Music Men Have Died By". It had the Marseillaise, Yankee Doodle, Dixie, and a bunch of national anthems. It also had the Internationale and the Horst Wessel Lied. Not a bad prop, I thought, just about as good as my fancy questionnaires.

Her voice reached me. "Let us stop playing games, Mr. Evans. Why are you here?"

I turned to look at her. It was a sensible question. I wished I had a plausible answer. Not having one, and not knowing exactly what was expected of me now, I resorted to doubletalk.

I tapped the record sleeve and asked, "Didn't you invite me, Miss Smith?"

"Who are you?"

"Who are you?" I asked. "And why are you keeping people awake nights with reactionary old songs played too loudly?"

"People?" she murmured. "And have *people* complained, Mr. Evans? People named Head, perhaps?"

"It could be," I said, wondering how long I could get away with playing it cagy.

"To you?" She watched me. "Then you must be a fairly important and influential person, Mr. Evans. If *people* can complain to you about minor annoyances and expect to have them attended to."

I said, snapping a fingernail against the record sleeve: "I wouldn't say this annoyance was minor. It could cause a lot of trouble, if someone else in the neighborhood should happen to recognize it."

I was still on the beam; this was obviously an attitude she'd expected. She had her answer ready: "Bah, these Americans! They make no effort to learn about their enemies. They are afraid to, lest their friends think them subversive. They talk loudly about Communism, but how many of them recognize the Internationale when they hear it? They complain peevishly about Fascism, and Nazism, but not one in a thousand, or ten thousand, recognizes the Horst Wessel Lied."

"Still, it's a risk," I said. It seemed safe to bear down a little, and I went on: "I think it would be better if you did not play this record again."

"A threat, Mr. Evans?" She came forward and took the cardboard envelope from my hand. She turned to get the record from the spindle and slipped it inside. She put the record on the shelf. "So. Not because you frighten me. Just because it has served its purpose."

"Which is?"

"To make contact," she said. "To make contact with someone in authority here. Perhaps you?"

"Perhaps," I said.

"I have credentials."

"Credentials?" I said. "What kind of credentials, and from whom?"

"From Argentina," she said. "From the Society for National Security, the SSN, of Argentina. Signed by—"

I dredged out of my memory what I'd read about fascist movements in Argentina. I made an impatient gesture, interrupting her, and said, "Argentina is full of hotheaded, irresponsible, swastika-waving fools! The Tacuara and the Guardia Whatsisname Nationale and now your SSN. Some of these idiots, I suppose, are capable of signing their names.

To anything. In any case, credentials can be forged. To whom were you supposed to present these so-called credentials, Miss Smith."

"In the first place, to a man who is dead," she said. "To a man who was to come here and take me to his superior. His, and I suppose, yours."

"Just like that," I said scornfully. "You'd shake hands and stroll across the street together to meet this man, I suppose."

She shook her head. "No," she said. "No, it was to be a difficult journey south to a secret destination in Mexico. I was warned to bring strong shoes and sturdy clothes, and a big hat and dark glasses for the sun. Other necessary equipment would be supplied by the courier. The rendezvous was to be the house of Mr. Ernest Head."

I studied her for a moment. I took a chance and commanded, "If you know so much, tell me the real name of Ernest Head."

"It used to be Schwarzkopf. Ernest Schwarzkopf. And his wife's name, in those days, was Gerda Landwehr."

"You've done your homework well," I said. "But then, an impostor would, wouldn't she?"

She drew herself up. "I was no impostor, Mr. Evans. Let me show you my—"

"I'm not interested in your credentials. I'm sure you have them or you wouldn't be trying to wave them under my nose. And I'm not about to travel to Argentina to check up on them. And if I put in a call, I'll have to ask you for the number, won't I? And I'm sure you'll have arranged to have the right person answer. Why didn't you present these pretty papers at the house over there?"

"When I telephoned, I was told to stay away," she said. "There was trouble, I was told. The courier had been followed on his previous trip. He'd had to run for the border. He had been caught, and had killed himself. It was not yet known how much of the local apparatus had been compromised. Everybody was sitting very tightly. I was a complication; I was not wanted; I was told to go away and not make things worse."

"And instead you bought this house and started playing the Horst Wessel with the window open."

"I asked to be put in touch with someone in authority. My request was refused." She faced me defiantly. "Your local troubles are not mine, Mr. Evans. I have my mission.

I have come a long way to carry it out. I was supposed to get cooperation here. I intend to get it, one way or another."

She was quite a girl. I said, "You could get something else, honey. Like a fist or a bullet." She did not react. I asked, "Just what's supposed to be your purpose in making this long and difficult journey?"

"That can be told to only one man," she said. "The man I am to meet in Mexico."

"His name?"

"You know his name."

"I know it," I said. "Let's hear if you do."

"In Germany he was known as Heinrich von Sachs." She looked up at me coldly. "Perhaps, in return, you had better tell me the name he uses in Mexico before we talk any more. So I have some way of knowing I'm talking to the right man."

I said, "You're in no position to make demands or set conditions, honey. But the name is Kurt Quintana." I saw her relax slightly, reassured. I went on, still playing it by ear, "And I don't believe Senor Quintana is interested in dealing with a bunch of South American hoodlums, male or female. And if he were, we'd have been notified that you were coming through here."

"You were notified," she said quickly, and I knew I'd made a mistake. "The message was sent and acknowledged."

"From here? We received no such message." I was bluffing hard now.

"No, the acknowledgement came from Mexico City." It was a break. I was still safe. She grimaced. "I am not responsible for the inefficient communications between your various cells, Mr. Evans. And I am neither a hoodlum nor am I a South American. There are a great many of us, of German extraction, down there; many of us who have memories in common."

I said scornfully, "Memories! Hell, you were learning the multiplication table when *Der Fuehrer* marched his troops into Poland. You were probably just learning about men when he . . ." I put a little catch into my voice . . . "when he died in the Bunker in Berlin. What memories can you have?"

"I was old enough to see both victory and defeat," she said. "I remember. The tradition lives, Mr. Evans. The new generation is ready. There are two continents here for the

taking. I do not believe General von Sachs will scorn our help. After all, for his great purpose, he was not above dealing with Fidelista communists in Costa Verde." Maybe I showed surprise that she'd have that information; maybe she just thought I did. Anyway, she went on with a confident little smile: "You see? I am no impostor. I know a great deal."

"Perhaps too much," I said harshly.

"Always the threats," she murmured. She took a step forward and placed her hands flat against the front of my shirt, and smiled up at me. "Would you hurt me, Mr. Evans? Would you beat me? Would you kill me?"

She was very good. And the man in the bedroom was pretty good, too, but not quite good enough. I'd heard him come in and take up his post. I was a hunter of sorts before I went into this line of work, and I'd waited in a good many stands, listening for the rustle in the nearby brush, the rap of a hoof or antler against a log or branch, that would tell me game was near. The only trouble was, I was pretty sure this game was stalking me.

Well, it didn't seem likely they'd go to all this trouble just to kill me; and you have to take a few risks now and then, if you want information. I looked down at Catherine Smith like a man getting certain ideas, and I reached out with finger and thumb and plucked at a little black bow of ribbon at her throat. The negligee fell open in front. I used both hands to slip it off her shoulders. She let her arms fall, and it dropped to the rug about her feet, leaving her clad only in an interesting black dual-purpose garment designed to give support both to the breasts above and the stockings below.

I suppose my grandmother would have spoiled everything by calling it a corset, being a prosaic old lady; Madison Avenue has undoubtedly invented a much more glamorous and seductive name for it. I'd never encountered one in actual use before, perhaps because my tastes normally run to lean girls who don't require so much support. It made a novel and stimulating picture. There was an old-fashioned air about it that was kind of sweet, if you know what I mean, reminiscent of Lillian Russell and Lily Langtry. I could have given it more attention if I had not heard the door opening behind me.

I couldn't help wondering if it was going to be a black-jack job or if he knew his stuff well enough to hit the right pressure point barehanded. It was distracting, but I managed to take the intriguingly half-naked Miss Smith into my arms in the crudely passionate way of the aroused male. Her lips responded to my kiss, her hands gripped me fiercely—and moved down suddenly to pin my arms to my sides. She was a strong girl. Then the needle went into my neck.

Whatever they were using in the hypo worked fast enough that I never knew when I hit the floor.

XII

I WAS IN A CAR for a while. It was hard to tell how long. I kept leaving, so to speak, and coming back. The car stopped. I was carried a very short distance. Then everything was peaceful and I slept for a while and woke up tied to a wooden chair in front of a pair of blinding headlights belonging to a station wagon, the shape of which looked vaguely familiar.

It was a garage long enough to take the big car and still leave some space in front. Perhaps the architect was expecting Detroit to make them even bigger in the future; or perhaps the man of the house was supposed to use the extra space for a workbench for his do-it-yourself projects. The garage was still in the process of construction. Raw ends of wiring stuck out of junction boxes here and there. Bags of cement and plaster were stored in one corner, along with other odds and ends of building materials.

I tested my bonds as a matter of routine. I didn't expect to find any slack in the cords or any weakness in the chair, and I didn't. It had been a smooth, pro job from the start. These were people who knew what they were doing. The problem was finding out just what the hell that was.

"He is awake."

It was Catherine Smith's husky voice. Her shape came between me and the headlights. After a little I could make out that she'd got out of her sexy pinup costume and into a loose flowered blouse and tight white shorts, still not a picture of demure innocence.

"How do you feel, Mr. Evans?" she asked.

"Frustrated," I said. "Things were just getting interesting, as I recall. What happens now?"

"You talk," she said.

"About what?"

"You tell us where to find Heinrich von Sachs, or if you prefer, Kurt Quintana."

I suppose I should have expected it. After all, I was supposed to be a mysterious Nazi character with influence and authority, if she really believed that. The question was, what did it make her?

I said, "Go to hell, honey."

Her eyes narrowed. "I am not bluffing, Mr. Evans."

Well, that was what I had to prove, or disprove. If she really wasn't bluffing, if she really didn't know where Heinrich was, and really thought I did, then I was wasting my time on her. But there were things about her story I didn't buy, the Argentina part for one. It sounded like one of those cover stories that are carefully designed to sound plausible and be hard to check. Besides, I'm pretty good at spotting accents, particularly Spanish accents. I've lived with them in New Mexico, off and on, since I was a boy. She should have had some trace of one if she'd spent a lot of time in Spanish-speaking Argentina, and she didn't. I couldn't identify the faint accent that flavored her English, but it wasn't *Español*.

"Go to hell," I repeated bravely. "Whatever your needle expert's cooking up back in the corner, have him trot it out. He'll find it's a lot easier to stick a man from behind than to make him talk."

She hesitated. Then she held out her hand toward the man outside the lights, the man I hadn't yet seen who was presumably named Herman Smith, or at least went by that name, her alleged father. She snapped her fingers impatiently when nothing was handed her at once. So she was going to do the work herself. I suppose this made her a dreadful person, in conventional terms; but it had been a long time since I'd dealt in conventional terms. It increased my respect for her. I mean, I don't go for these delicate types, male or female, who want the cattle branded but can't bear to touch the iron themselves.

The man came into the glare of the lights holding a

cheap new soldering iron. The cord ran off into the darkness somewhere. The tool had obviously never been used before; you could smell the store finish burning off it.

The man was considerably older than I. He had grizzled black hair and a face like an eroded farm. There was a big blade of a nose, a thin, almost lipless mouth, and a bony chin. His eyes, when he looked at me, were shiny and expressionless, but I didn't gather he felt a great deal of sympathy for my predicament. He was wearing dark wash pants and a white shirt with the collar open and the sleeves rolled up. I caught the hint of a gun under the armpit. He'd have to get past at least two buttons to reach it there, but in summer, in the coatless southwest, there aren't too many places a man can pack a concealed firearm.

He gave the hot soldering iron to Catherine, and came over to unfasten my sport shirt and pull it down as far as my tied hands and the back of the chair would let him, preparing the patient for the operation. He stepped back into the darkness. Catherine came forward.

"Von Sachs," she said quietly. "Where does he have his headquarters, Mr. Evans? We know it's south of the border in Mexico, but where?"

"Try scopolamine, honey," I said. "That mail-order gadget won't get you anywhere."

"Von Sachs," she repeated. "Where is Heinrich von Sachs?"

"You're taking a chance that close, honey," I said. "I used to be the champion spitter of Santa Fe County, New Mexico. I'll put it right in your eye. . . . Ahhh!"

After that, it got a little rough. I mean, it was worse than hitting your thumb with a heavy hammer or dropping a brick on your toe because it didn't stop. It was about like having a clumsy, persistent dentist working on you without Novocain. People have stood that and I stood this, but I don't pretend I was heroic about it. I grunted and sweated as it went on; I even considered screaming occasionally but decided against it. Things were tough enough without adding a gag to my discomforts.

"Von Sachs! Where is Heinrich von Sachs?"

After a while I passed out. I couldn't have been unconscious long, because when I opened my eyes she'd only stepped back a pace, waiting for me to revive. I noticed she wasn't as pretty as she had been. Sweat had turned her face shiny and streaked her make-up. Her big, fancy hairdo was starting to fall apart. She made no attempt to repair the damage. Perhaps she wasn't even aware of it. More likely she just let her wild-woman appearance alone because she knew she looked more scary that way. When she saw my eyes open, she lifted the iron and stepped forward again.

"Katerina."

It was the voice of the man behind me. Catherine glanced his way irritably.

"What is it, Max?"

So his name was Max, not Herman Smith. I'd learned something, after all. It hardly seemed worth the effort.

"It is no good," Max said. "In a week, maybe. In a month, yes. One can break any man in a month. But the construction crew will be here in the morning."

"I will burn his eyes out if he does not talk!" she said violently. "I will. . . ."

She described the other ingenious things she would do to me. She was talking for effect, of course, to intimidate me, but there was no doubt in my mind now that her basic emotion was genuine. She wasn't bluffing, certainly. She really wanted to know where von Sachs could be found. She really thought I could tell her. She obviously didn't have the information we wanted, since she was searching for it herself.

It seemed that I'd come a long, painful way for a negative answer. I'd eliminated a possibility, that was all. As far as the job was concerned, I was back where I'd started. That wasn't strictly correct, either. I'd started from a comfortable motel room. I wasn't quite back there yet. I tried to think of the right card to play next. Now I had to convince these pleasant sadists, not only that I didn't have what they wanted, but that I'd do them no harm if they let me go. I wished that my head were clearer and that I didn't feel quite so much like being sick to my stomach.

Catherine had finished her catalog of horrors. She was back on her where-is-von-Sachs? kick. As she stepped forward, raising the soldering iron to continue the treatment, the small side door of the garage slammed open and Sheila stepped in, holding a little .38 revolver that, to my prejudiced eyes, looked prettier than any rose.

XIII

In a tv show, that would have been it. In real life, unfortunately, there's a little more to a daring rescue than just pointing a gun at the villain and telling him to behave —particularly when there are two villains and they know their villainy.

Sheila should have shot, of course. She should have dropped one of them instantly, and maybe the other would have stayed put; but it's the hardest thing in the world to teach the recruits. Even during the war, some of them never learned that you didn't wait to inspect the church and count the congregation, you just kicked in the door, tossed in a grenade, and went in behind the explosion with your machine pistol firing. . . .

They didn't wait for her to make up her mind. I saw Catherine make a catlike leap for the shelter of the car; she might not be built lean, but she moved lean. I heard Max come for me, since I was the best protection within his reach. I heard shirt buttons go as he went for the armpit gun. I managed to dump the chair on its side and my timing was good; we connected and got tangled up on the floor. He rolled free. There was nothing I could do about that, tied as I was. I'd made my small contribution to the cause. Catherine reached the switch and the station wagon headlights went out.

I lay in the dark and listened to them jockeying for position around me and the car. They were trying to get each other located. Sheila still had the advantage. She knew where I was; she knew which way not to shoot. Max and Catherine had to identify a target before firing or risk killing each other. I didn't think, however, it would take them long to get a systematic campaign under way.

I thought about this, and I thought about a small, relatively inexperienced girl crouching somewhere in the dark with a revolver in her hand. I thought about various things that had happened tonight that I hadn't had time enough, or sense enough, to add together before.

"Skinny," I said, "don't answer, don't move, but listen. You see the open door you came in by. There's a patch of lighted floor. Got it? Throw your gun there."

I heard a shocked gasp somewhere to the right. I heard somebody move a little off to the left, presumably to get a clear shot at the source of the gasp, if it should reveal itself again.

I said, "Hold everything, everybody. Let's not make a massacre of this. Sheila, that's an order. Toss your gun over there where they can see it."

There was complete silence for some forty to sixty seconds. Then the short-barreled .38 hit the lighted patch of floor with a solid sound. A man's hand showed in the light for an instant, raked it up, and vanished.

I said, "Fine. Now, Sheila, walk over there slowly and stand with your hands in plain sight where they can see you."

There was another long pause. I heard her stir. She came into sight and stood there, silhouetted in the gray rectangle of the doorway.

I said, "Your move, Miss Smith."

Abruptly, the car lights came on. They showed Max flat on the floor not far from Sheila, covering her with a gun in each hand. He looked kind of silly in the light. Catherine came around the side of the car, brushing dust off her shorts. She had a small automatic pistol in her hand. I speculated on where she might have had it concealed. There was no room to spare inside the shorts, but of course the blouse offered some interesting hiding places.

I said to Sheila, "Now you can come over here and cut me loose. I think there's still a knife in my right pants pocket—"

"Don't move, girl!" That was two-gun Max, getting up.

I said, "Don't be silly. Come on, Sheila. Oh, and pick up your gun from the nice man on the way. He can unload it first if he's scared."

"Katerina!"

I looked at Catherine. She was watching me, frowning slightly. She was a little behind me in her thinking, but she was catching up fast. I saw her come to a decision.

"Give the little girl back her toy, Max," she said. "Leave the cartridges. It is all right." She smiled at me. "You look very foolish lying there. . . . It is all right, Max!" she snapped, seeing that her man still hadn't turned over the gun. "Would he have disarmed her in the first place if he were what we think? There has obviously been a mistake."

She tucked the little automatic away inside the flowered blouse somewhere, and knelt beside me to cut me free. While I was getting to my feet stiffly, she went over to the fender of the car, where a white purse lay. She opened the purse and took out a tube of some kind of ointment and tossed it to me.

"Use that. It has an anesthetic that will reduce the pain."

I stuck the tube in my pocket and buttoned my shirt courageously. "Pain?" I said. "What pain? Hell, I juggle red-hot pokers for kicks. I drink flaming brandy; I walk on burning coals to keep my tootsies warm. Who the hell are you, Miss Smith? And don't give me any more of that Argentina jazz. If you really had a proposition from the swastika kids down there for Heinrich von Sachs, you wouldn't start out by cooking a guy you thought was one of his henchmen piecemeal. So let's hear who you really are. A little honesty, please, Miss Smith."

"First, who are you?" she asked.

"I am an agent of the government of the United States of America, God help it," I said, having decided the only way to play this now was straight. Well, reasonably straight. "Apparently I'm trying to find the same man you are."

"You thought *I* would know?"

"You were playing a very interesting tune. I thought it worth investigating. We seem to've been working at cross purposes. Your turn. Identification, please."

"I am an agent of. . . ." She hesitated. "I cannot give you the name of the organization, Mr. Evans, or the country from which it operates. I am sorry. You would be duty bound to tell your government. I can tell you this much, however: it is our mission to bring Heinrich von Sachs to justice for his crimes against humanity."

"Sure," I said. "That figures. But it makes things kind of awkward. I suppose you want him alive."

"We are not murderers, Mr. Evans."

I touched my chest gingerly. "You don't seem to have many other scruples. Unfortunately we seem to be operating under contradictory orders. My solution to the von Sachs problem is supposed to be immediate and permanent. Are there any circumstances under which we might, say, compromise?"

She hesitated, and said with obvious reluctance, "Well, if it proves absolutely impossible to take the man prisoner. . . ." She stopped. After a moment she said, "Perhaps we could waive the question of jurisdiction temporarily. We both want von Sachs. It will be difficult enough to get him without fighting each other. If we were to combine our resources. . . ."

"Resources," I said. "Your soldering iron and my chest?"

"I am sorry. It was a mistake."

I said, "I wouldn't join forces with you, you sadistic slut, if you had the map of von Sachs' hideout tucked in your brassiere along with that toy pistol!"

She smiled. "Now you feel better, having called me names, don't you?"

I grinned. "Lots better. What do you know that's of any use to me."

"What do *you* know, Mr. Evans?"

I sighed. "All right. Gentlemen first. I know the only road down into the area. I've been down it myself once, a long time ago. I have the latest reports on its condition."

"I understand it is not a very good road."

I said, "Easy does it, honey. I'll tell you all about it, but first you give a little."

She shrugged. "Very well. I have a cover story that will get me in to General von Sachs once I know where to find him. There *have* been overtures made to him by people in Argentina. I think I can make him accept me as one of them, long enough to serve our purpose. I also know somebody who knows where to find him. It was for this person I was playing the music when you blundered in and very cleverly made me think you were a more promising candidate."

I watched her face closely and asked, "Ernest Head?"

She nodded quickly. "Yes. Of course. Ernst Schwarzkopf. The question is how to approach him."

"Approach," I said. "You put it so delicately, doll. You mean catch him and sweat him, don't you? Like you did me."

She shook her head. "No, that is a last resource. If we try to make him talk and fail, we have lost everything. I think we should try to make him run. That is what I have been trying to accomplish." She made an impatient gesture. "If it were just a matter of capture and torture, do you think I would have been wasting my time playing the phonograph? But I was hoping I could make him run so that Max and I could follow. Where else would he go? I still think he can be made to do it. A little more pressure should suffice. And with three to take turns watching— you two and Max—there should be no chance of his eluding us. We will let him lead us to von Sachs. Now what about that road? Can it be traveled in an ordinary car or will we need a jeep?"

"When I went down, years ago, we used a pickup truck," I said. "But my information is that the road's in good shape this year, and a passenger car should make it all right. Of course that applies only to the dirt road south from Antelope Wells. What kind of a track turns off it into the Nacimiento Mountains is anybody's guess. However, von Sachs isn't likely to pack his stuff in by mountain goat. If he's got any kind of big operation going back in there, in the guise of an archaeological expedition, the access trail can't be too difficult."

Catherine Smith frowned. "I don't think much of your contribution, Mr. Evans. A few questions at Antelope Wells would have given me as much. It seems to me this is going to be a very one-sided partnership, in which Max and I supply most of the information and run most of the risks."

"Sure," I said. "How well do you and your friend know this part of the North American continent, Miss Smith?"

"What do you mean?"

"I mean, I was brought up in these parts. I know these mountains and deserts, honey. Give me half a lead and I can tell you where von Sachs has got to be. Give me four wheels and an engine and I can take you there. How much back-country driving have you done, either of you? You look like city operators to me. When I say that road's in good shape, I don't mean it's a six-lane turnpike. It's still a Mexican desert road. You're going to need me. Don't kid yourself you aren't."

"I see." She smiled cynically. "So now that road is suddenly so terrible it takes an expert to drive it." She shrugged. "Oh, very well. Max will keep an eye on Ernest Head tonight. You two will cover him tomorrow. I will see that he hears the record often enough to keep old memories fresh in his mind until he can stand it no longer."

I grinned. "You're such a sweet girl; you have such kind thoughts. All right, it's a deal. We find von Sachs; after that we flip a coin, or something, to see who gets him."

I regarded her for a moment. "Of course, if anybody tries a doublecross, all bets are off."

She smiled. "Of course."

"Okay. We'll take over from Max in the morning. Now, where are we and how do we get out of here?"

Presently I was driving the station wagon away from there with Sheila beside me. It took me a little while to get oriented, until I realized that we were only a few blocks from Catherine's house, in an area of new construction.

"Where's your car, Skinny?" I asked without turning my head. Under the circumstances, I wasn't moving anything that wasn't absolutely necessary.

"Turn right at the next corner . . . Eric."

"What?"

"You don't really trust that . . . that blonde praying mantis, do you?"

I made the effort to glance at her. "Trust her? A pretty, sweet, gentle little girl like that? Why shouldn't I trust her?" I grimaced. "I trust her to doublecross us at the first glimmer of an opportunity. Do you think I'd have made a deal with her if I didn't?"

XIV

WHEN I REACHED the motel, I saw that the blue Volkswagen had beat me home. I hadn't felt up to any fancy driving. Besides, I'd had to stop at a pay phone and put in a long-distance call to Washington asking for full reports on a woman who called herself Catherine Smith, a man who called himself Max, and a couple of married people locally known as Mr. And Mrs. Ernest Head, who'd in the past gone by other names, specified. I'd paid for all those names. I figured I might as well go through the motions of feeding them into the machinery, although I had doubts whether the information would get out to me in time to be of much use.

I saw Sheila get out of her little car as I turned in off

the street. She came up beside me as I parked the station wagon.

"Are you all right?" she whispered. "When you didn't arrive right behind me, I got worried. Come on. I'd better look after those burns."

She opened the car door and started to help me out, but she remembered her neurosis about heterosexual contacts and checked herself short of touching me. Or perhaps she just realized that a two-hundred-pound man has to be in pretty bad shape before he takes kindly to being helped out of a car by a hundred-pound girl. She did take the motel key out of my hand and open that door for me and close it behind me.

I said, "What the hell are you bucking for, Skinny? The title of little mother of the year? Hell, I've singed myself worse than this lighting a cigarette."

She looked startled and injured; then she laughed. "All right. Be brave. Be heroic. Do you want a drink?"

"Sure."

"Ice?"

"If there's any left."

"It's all melted," she said, investigating. "I'll get some more. I'll be right back."

I started to register a gentlemanly protest, but she'd already taken the cardboard bucket and slipped out of the room. I sat down on the bed and took off my shirt. After examining the battlefield, I came to the conclusion that regardless of how it felt, it wasn't really the scene of a major catastrophe. The only burn that went deep was on the shoulder. Elsewhere I'd merely lost a little skin. The fact that it hurt like hell was, to a tough undercover operative of my courageous and stoical nature, irrelevant. At least it was supposed to be.

I took from my pocket the tube of ointment Catherine Smith had given me. I was sitting there reading the label and feeling sorry for myself when Sheila let herself back in quietly. She put the ice bucket on the dresser, came over to look, and snatched the tube from my hand.

"You're not going to use *that*?"

"Why not?"

"I wouldn't trust her to give me anything but syphilis!"

I said, "That's probably the one thing she can't give you, Skinny. At least I'm under the impression VD doesn't work like that."

"You know what I mean!"

"Sure," I said. "She's a terrible person. Okay? Now may I have that drink?"

Sheila tossed the ointment on the bed and marched off across the room. She was still wearing the summery print dress with a good deal of skirt and not much bodice, but she'd exchanged her high-heeled shoes for a pair of white sneakers more suitable for playing detective. They made her look like a high-school girl. I watched her fix my drink and wondered why looking at her gave me a funny tight feeling in the throat that the sexy Miss Smith in her black lingerie hadn't elicited at all. Well, not much. I decided that I was getting old and paternal and protective—or real expert at kidding myself.

I spoke to her back. "I haven't thanked you for the timely help."

To my surprise, I saw her wince as if I'd said something harsh and cruel. She turned swiftly to look at me.

"Don't!" she breathed. "Don't make fun of me!"

"I wasn't—"

"I know I made a fool of myself!" Her voice was low. "Don't you think I know it? You'd have done better to pick a green kid to help you. He'd have remembered how to come through a door with a gun. That's what you're thinking, isn't it? I don't blame you! But you don't have to be sarcastic!"

I said, "No sarcasm was intended. As it happened, everything turned out for the best. There are no shots to explain, no dead bodies to dispose of. And you did turn up right on the dot. I was wondering how the hell to talk myself out of there, when you barged in." After a little pause, I said, "Of course, you're not supposed to shadow me without instructions, doll."

She came over with a glass and put it into my hand. "And you're not supposed to send me to bed like a child because you think I look tired. If I'd been a man, husky and healthy, you'd have had me covering you tonight, wouldn't you? It would have been routine. So I did." After a moment, she picked up the ointment tube, punched a hole in the end, squeezed out a little of the salve, and smelled it suspiciously. "I suppose this stuff really is all right to use. How do you feel?"

"I'm all right," I said. "You can't hurt us seasoned veterans of the hush-hush service. We're all made of rhinoceros hide and old iron. . . . Ouch!"

She'd started to apply the stuff to the burn on my shoulder

just as if she were an ordinary girl instead of a mental case with a thing about being touched by, or touching, men. A little startled, I couldn't help stealing a look at her face. It looked kind of pink and white and determined. She was concentrating very hard on what she was doing and not meeting my eyes at all. The only trouble was, she wasn't very gentle.

I said, "Hey, take it easy."

"You!" she said softly. "You and that overdeveloped bitch in her little peekaboo foundation garment. Black! And stockings, sheer black nylon stockings, at this time of year! How obvious can you get?" She started on my chest. "Lean back a little."

"Why, Skinny," I said, "you're a peeping Tom, that's what you are."

"The window was open. Did you have to kiss her?"

I said, "It says on the label a light application, doll. A vigorous massage is not indicated. This town seems to be just crawling with sadistic females." The pressure eased somewhat. I glanced at her again. "What was I supposed to do, carry on an intellectual conversation with the dame in her underwear while I waited for her partner to fight his way out of the bedroom and clobber me? And what's it to you, anyway?"

It was meant to be light and casual, but my casual touch didn't seem to be functioning tonight. Her hand stopped moving abruptly. After a moment she stepped back and stared at me oddly. Her eyes were wide and yellow. She looked down at the sticky fingers of her right hand, and at the tube in her left hand, also sticky. She looked around for something to wipe them on and didn't find anything. She dropped the tube, and whirled, and ran for the door.

I was on my feet by this time, but she'd have beat me out if the doorknob hadn't been reluctant and her hands hadn't been slippery; that gave me a chance to get across the room. I caught her by the bare shoulders and shoved the door shut with my foot. She became perfectly still.

"Don't touch me!"

"Cut it out," I said. "We're all through with that don't-touch-me routine, remember? It's gone the way of the no-talk bit."

"Let me go," she whispered. "Please!"

I let her go. She turned to face me, holding her sticky hands away from her dress.

"I'm sorry," she breathed. "I was . . . just being silly and melodramatic. I'm all right now."

"Sure."

"Dr. Stern explained it to me," she said. "He called it a transference, I think. That's all it is. Just a transference."

"Sure," I said. "Just a transference."

"It's perfectly natural," she said. "I mean, it isn't your fault. After all, you saved my life."

"Me and twenty-three other people."

"They didn't all get blisters on their hands carrying me to safety. They didn't . . . didn't feed me milkshakes clear across the continent and talk to me as if I were a person and not a shattered wreck. They didn't get me out of that place where those ghouls were going to take my mind apart like a broken clock and put in all kinds of bright new springs and wheels I didn't want. . . . Let me go to my room, Eric," she whispered. "Please."

"Sure," I said.

She didn't move. "Damn you," she whispered, "you're just an ordinary man, a little taller than average. You're not really very nice. I mean, you aren't even above arranging things so you can make a pass at a woman in the line of duty. Duty! I saw you! And you're not very brave, you wiggle and groan like anybody else when it hurts. I heard you. I don't know why I . . . I mean, there's nothing special about you. I don't know why any woman would want . . . Eric."

"Yes."

"Kick me out. Make me go. It's just a transference. A simple psychological phenomenon. It isn't fair to let me stand here making a spectacle of myself. It isn't fair to laugh."

"I'm not laughing," I said.

The room was suddenly very quiet. She shook her head minutely, looking up at me. Then she was coming forward, or I was, I forget how it happened. Then we stopped. There were the practical aspects to consider.

One of us laughed, maybe both, I forget; and Sheila turned quickly, presenting her back to me. "If you're not going to kick me out," she breathed, "if you're not, then I think you'd better help me off with my dress before . . . before we get that stuff all over it."

XV

I WOKE UP SCARED. I couldn't at first remember what I'd done, only that it was unforgivable. Then I sat up quickly and looked around. I was alone in the room. There wasn't a sign of Sheila. She'd gone during the night, leaving none of her belongings behind.

I pulled on my pants and crossed the room and looked at myself in the mirror. The only satisfactory part of the image was the pattern of burns and blisters, which were all right as far as they went, but they didn't go half far enough. A heel like you, I told myself, should be trussed hand and foot and revolved slowly over a bed of glowing charcoal, like a roast pig. Any creep who'd take advantage of the irrational hero-worship and gratitude of a sick and confused little girl for whom he'd been made responsible. . . .

A knock on the door made me jump. "Mr. Evans?"

It was Sheila's voice. I got over there and pulled the door open. She was standing outside with a paper cup of coffee in each hand, looking remarkably healthy and unconfused in the shortsleeved white shirt and tan cotton pants in which she'd crossed the country with me some weeks earlier, now crisp and clean again. Despite the pants, which are my least favorite feminine garment, she looked more like a woman and less like a disturbed child than any time since I'd known her.

She stepped past me. I closed the door. She was looking at me hard when I turned. "What's the matter, darling?" she asked. "You look awful. Are you having some kind of a shock reaction? Let me look at that shoulder."

"The hell with the shoulder," I said. "Are you all right?"

She frowned slightly. "Why shouldn't I be all right . . . Oh." She looked up at me and laughed. "Heavens, have you been having an attack of conscience, or something?"

"Or something," I said grimly.

She said, "Here. Drink your coffee and try to be sensible."

I said, "I'm sensible as hell, now. But Dr. Tommy would have me shot, and quite justifiably, if he knew—"

"Don't be ridiculous," she said. "Dr. Stern is an idiot if he thinks. . . . What *does* he think?"

"Well, I'd say seduction is the last medicine in the world he'd prescribe for this particular patient."

"That's what I said," she murmured, "he's an idiot! I've been married, darling. I've been. . . . Well, it's not as if I were an innocent virgin, is it? On the record, that's the one thing in the world I'm not. Why should it hurt me to go to bed with a man I like, for a change?" She laughed. "Anyway, who seduced whom?"

I looked down at her, reflecting that things and people never seemed to turn out quite the way you expected, particularly people.

"You're a shameless wench, Skinny," I said.

"Of course," she said calmly. "What did you think I was? All you had to do was look at the file and you'd know that after all that I had to be a shameless wench, or dead." A little hardness had come into her voice. "Don't worry about hurting me, darling. It's been tried by experts, and I don't mean just the ones in Costa Verde. I'll tell you about my marriage sometime. It was a dilly. I'm not really fragile, you know. Just because I'm not built like a . . . like a brick outhouse doesn't mean. . . ." She stopped.

I grinned. "Here we go again."

She laughed and said, "Honest, I wasn't really thinking of Catherine Smith when I said that. Well, maybe I was. . . . Eric?"

"Yes."

"Last night I . . . I said a lot of silly things, didn't I? Don't take them seriously, please."

I regarded her for a moment. "Sure," I said.

She went on quickly, "I mean, we're not going to be silly and talk a lot of nonsense about love. After all those weeks of being an animal in a cage, I was ready to . . . to attach myself to the first person who treated me as a human being. You don't have to feel, well, obligated. I'll get over it." She gulped her coffee and glanced at her watch. "Well, I'd better get going."

"Where?"

She looked surprised. "Why, one of us has to get over to Saguaro Heights and relieve Max, remember."

"That's right, I'd almost forgotten." I hesitated. "Okay. But watch yourself."

"What do you mean?"

"They're probably playing us for suckers," I said. "Catherine and Max. That's all right. That's what we want. For one thing, it cancels the mutual-assistance pact, and I'd much rather have the other party pull the doublecross. It's a matter of principle. I'm a very high-principled guy. Sometimes."

She smiled and stopped smiling. "You're being clever," she said. "And you don't want to tell me."

"I hope I'm being clever," I said. "And I'm not telling you because not knowing will save you some acting. Besides, I could be absolutely wrong."

She was silent for a moment. Then she said, "Of course, these people do have a legitimate claim to von Sachs, if you want to put it like that."

"They are entitled to have him arrested legally and extradited legally, if they can. They have no legitimate right to kidnap him for his past crimes, any more than we have to kill him for what he's cooking up for the future. We're all operating equally far outside the law." I looked down at her small, scrubbed, neatly lipsticked face. "And just keep in mind that even if their motives are perfectly wonderful, they aren't really very nice people. Keep your eyes open."

Sheila checked in a couple of times during the morning. When I drove by at noon to find her, she was sitting in her little blue car watching the automobile agency where Ernest Head worked. It was a busy, bright street near the center of Tucson. I tapped my horn lightly as I passed and turned the next corner and found a vacant meter at which to park. Presently Sheila got into the station wagon beside me. I moved some packages to give her room.

"Nothing," she said. "As I told you on the phone, he drove to work right after I got on the job. He's been in there all morning. He'll probably go out for lunch pretty soon, or maybe he'll go home. It's Saturday. Maybe he only works half a day." She paused. "I was followed earlier this morning."

"Who? Max?"

She nodded. "I think he was just checking up on me. White Falcon station wagon, Arizona plates. Regular tires in front, mud-and-snow treads behind."

"Sounds like they're ready for some tough driving. Or think they are."

Sheila glanced at me curiously. "Why did you tell Miss Smith the road was good? That's not what you told me."

I said, "If she gets herself a jeep, she'll have no trouble, and we'll need a jeep to keep up with her. If she goes in her own car, she may run into difficulties that we can take advantage of. At least she'll have to take it very slow and easy. It'll be a lot harder for her to pull a fast one. I don't want her in a jeep. Okay?"

Sheila laughed. "It must be nice to be so clever," she murmured.

"Is Max around now?" I asked.

"No. I'm almost certain, anyway. What's all this stuff?" She looked curiously at the packages on the seat.

"Just some things we may need later. I've been laying in supplies," I said. "We're ready to roll as soon as we know where we're going and get the rifle sighted in. It's in back. I thought we'd grab a hamburger and go take care of that little chore."

"What about Ernest?" she asked.

"He'll keep," I said. "Don't worry about Ernest."

She studied my face for a moment. "I suppose you know what you're doing."

"Sure," I said. "Making you curious as hell, that's what I'm doing. Go back to your car and drive straight ahead, but give me a couple of minutes first to get around the block behind you. I want to make sure Max doesn't see us taking off; it might worry him. I'll pass you when I'm satisfied we're in the clear. . . ."

Nobody tailed us. We had a hamburger at a drive-in, and headed out into the desert, where I'd earlier scouted an arroyo where we could improvise a private hundred-yard rifle range with a high dirt bank for a backstop. I set up some targets and had Sheila bring down the rifle and fire a few rounds at short range to see where the gun was shooting. We got the telescopic sight roughly centered, so the shots would at least go on the paper at a hundred yards, before we backed off and started shooting for group with the various loads I'd brought along.

"You're going to have to do most of the work, Skinny," I said. "My shoulder's in no condition to take a pounding. Give her five with each bullet weight. Hold as close as you can, exactly the same way every time."

Watching her shoot, I was glad I hadn't bought a Magnum. Even a standard .30-06 is a lot of gun for a small girl to shoot from rest, prone, where the body can't rock back with the recoil but has to stay and take the punishment. I squatted behind her with a pair of binoculars I'd picked up. They weren't bad glasses, but they weren't strong enough to really distinguish bullet holes at that range; and I was more interested in watching the girl, anyway.

The sun was bright on her short-cut hair as she lay there, firing steadily. I could remember when it had been even shorter, hacked and ragged. Well, that had nothing to do with sighting in a rifle, or with her marksmanship in general. What was important was that she seemed to know that she was doing. They all get rifle training, but it doesn't always take. After she'd finished, we went down to inspect the targets. I put my pocket ruler across the best group.

"Four and a quarter inches with the 150-grain load," I said. "A bolt-action rifle that won't group within two inches at a hundred yards isn't worth having, and we ought to get one and a half even with factory ammunition. Is that as close as you can hold?"

"They all felt good," she said. "They should all have been right together."

"You don't mind if I check you?"

"No," she said stiffly. "No, of course I don't mind."

"Don't get mad, Skinny," I said. "I've got to know if it's you or the gun that's spreading them out like that. Just because you're swell in bed doesn't necessarily mean you're hell on the rifle range, too."

She stared at me, startled and indignant; then she laughed. We went back to a hundred yards and I fired five. It was no fun at all. The burn was in exactly the wrong place. My group beat hers by only a quarter of an inch, good enough for the male ego but no prize in the accuracy department. After checking, and putting up fresh targets, I got out the tools and took the gun apart. She sat on the ground beside me to watch.

"I think the stock has warped a little," I said. "They often do on these light rifles. It's supposed to be a free-floating barrel without any wood contact, but I think we're getting some pressure here that's throwing it off. We'll just ream out the barrel channel a bit and put in a few cardboard shims to free things up around the action. The magazine isn't supposed to bind like this, either." I glanced at her. "They didn't teach you anything about this, did they?"

"No," she said. "All they did was make us shoot."

"As a matter of fact, I picked it up as a kid," I said. "I always used to be crazy about guns. And knives and swords and all the rest of the stuff that tickles a kid's bloodthirsty imagination. That was before World War II, of course. They picked me out of the Army after a couple of months of that and put me into this outfit. We had us quite a war."

"And afterward?" she asked.

"I said the hell with it and got married, but it didn't take. Well, that isn't quite right. I wasn't allowed to tell the girl my wartime experiences, and everything was swell for a good many years, until one day she discovered what kind of a monster was sharing the master bedroom with her. She's out in Nevada now, married to a rancher."

"She must be a fool," Sheila said.

I looked up and grinned. "Watch that transference, Skinny." I shook my head. "It wasn't a question of brains but of stomach. Beth's a bright enough girl. She's just allergic to gore, is all. I guess she felt, too, that I'd been holding out on her, and of course I had, under orders." I started putting the rifle back together. "Well, that ought to improve things slightly."

"Eric."

"Yes," I said.

Sheila's voice was low. "Have you ever thought of marrying again? Somebody . . . somebody who knows all about you and doesn't care?"

I looked at her sitting in the sunshine with a lot of desert behind her. "Don't go off half-cocked," I said. "It's a simple psychological phenomenon. You'll get over it. You said so yourself."

She hesitated. "Have you . . . have you got a girl?"

"There's a nice lady in Texas. Pretty, too. We sometimes get together when I'm on leave."

"Does *she* know the kind of work you do?"

I said, "I met her on a job. She was kind of accidentally involved. She knows. But she's had four husbands and isn't looking for a fifth, if that's what you're driving at."

"Is she . . . really good-looking?"

"And young. And rich," I said. "She's also a pretty swell person, in a cool, sophisticated sort of way. What do you want me to say, that I go around with a real creep?"

Sheila laughed and stopped laughing. "Do you love her?" she asked.

I said, "Hold this while I try to match up. . . . Hold it steady. Thanks. I thought we weren't going to talk any nonsense about love."

Sheila said, "Don't keep throwing my words back at me. I had a husband once. He was a beast. A louse. Any word you can think of. I mean, really a beast, physically, mentally, and morally, only it didn't show up until after we were married, or maybe I was just too damn innocent to know the symptoms. I mean the kind of man that . . . that makes you want to wipe all men off the face of the earth, if you're a woman. So I divorced him and joined this organization, hoping they could give me some work along those lines. Extermination was for me. I'd been very much in love, you understand. I was terribly disillusioned and very bitter."

I said, "Dr. Tommy has a theory about you that goes something like that. Of course, he's got a fancy sexual angle, like all headshrinkers. They're afraid Papa Freud will disown them if they don't."

She glanced at me warily. "What did Dr. Stern tell you about me?"

"Well, there was something about a childhood trauma—of a sexual nature, of course. Tommy apparently didn't have it treed yet, but he was baying on the trail. He thinks it's the secret key to all your personality difficulties."

She laughed. "I had a perfectly normal childhood, thanks. I was never followed through the park by a scary man who exposed himself, or molested in the stairwell by the janitor. Honest."

"You'll break Tommy's heart," I said. "Then there was your unsatisfactory marriage. He says it broke up with charges of brutality on one side and frigidity on the other."

She grimaced. "Don't you know that any time a man wants to hurt a woman publicly, he calls her frigid? How does Dr. Stern reconcile my supposed frigidity with the fact that I went down to Costa Verde deliberately to . . . to seduce a bearded bandit I'd never seen?"

"You were trying to prove something by putting yourself on a spot, says Tommy. You wanted to demonstrate, to yourself and everybody else, that your husband was a damn liar. And Dr. Tommy's theory is that you proved something, all right: the wrong thing. He thinks that what happened is that you panicked when El Fuerte started making amorous advances and gave yourself and the show away."

Sheila didn't look at me. "And what do you think?"

I said, "Don't be silly. This is Mr. Henry Evans, honey, the guy you spent the night with, remember? We'll consider the frigidity theory disproved. But that still leaves the question of just what happened down there to trip you up."

"Why, I simply goofed," she said, frankly. "Maybe I *was* a little scared. Not of El Fuerte's amorous advances. Just of being caught and killed."

"It's normal," I said. "What was the goof?"

"I got the gun, all right," she said. "His gun. After inviting me into his hut as we'd planned for him to do, he'd chivalrously taken off his belt and holster so I wouldn't get bruised by all the buckles and hardware. I got the pistol, all right, but you know the grip safety on that big .45 automatic. If you don't hold the gun just right, that spring-loaded gizmo doesn't release, and nothing happens when you pull the trigger even though the thumb-safety is off. I have a small hand and, as I say, maybe I was a little nervous. And he was fast, faster than you'd expect such a big man to be. After that initial delay, I never had a chance."

It was a good story, a plausible story. There isn't anybody working with firearms who hasn't, at some time in his career, fumbled a safety device and missed a shot. The only trouble was that I'd heard a lot of good, plausible stories: I knew she was lying. Something had happened down there that she was ashamed or afraid to tell me, probably just that she'd lost her nerve at the critical moment much more drastically than she cared to admit.

Well, it happens. I just wished she hadn't felt compelled to lie, as if I gave a damn how brave she had or had not been. I slipped the bolt back into the rifle and passed the weapon over.

"Let's finish the job and get out of this sun," I said. "Give me another five with the 150-grain load to see how she's grouping now and where she's putting them on the paper. Then we'll sight her in three inches high at a hundred yards. That'll put her just about on the button at two-fifty. How's your shoulder holding up?"

"It's all right," she said. "Eric, I—"

"What is it?"

"Nothing," she said. "Five shots, you said?"

"Five," I said.

"One day," she said brightly, "one day I'll fall for a man who'll settle for three-shot groups or do his own damn shooting."

XVI

ON THE WAY BACK to the motel, I stopped at a public phone booth to make a phone call. I had to get the number from the operator, as it was a new installation not yet listed in the book. After dialing, I let the ringing continue for a long time, but no one answered. Apparently neither Catherine Smith nor her alleged father were at home. Well, they wouldn't be if they were behaving as I hoped and expected them to.

When I reached the motel, Sheila's car was already parked in front of her unit. I hesitated, but there wasn't anything I had to say to her, and if she had anything to say to me, she'd had plenty of opportunity. To hell with her and her dark secrets, anyway. As I entered my room, the phone started to ring. I closed the door, picked up the instrument, and heard her voice on the line.

"Mr. Evans?" she said. "I'm sorry to interrupt you, Mr. Evans, you're probably busy, but—"

I stood perfectly still, holding the instrument tightly. There were three words she could have used: disturb, bother, and interrupt. I'd always thought interrupt was a bad one, hard to fit naturally into an ordinary greeting, but that was the trouble code we were using, regardless.

I said slowly, repeating the word so she'd know I'd got it, "You're not interrupting anything, Miss Summerton. I just came in the door; I haven't started on my paper work yet. What can I do for you?"

She started to speak. Her voice sounded perfectly steady. I listened, thinking hard. The three code words are variations on the same theme. The first means, *I'm in trouble, save yourself.* The second means, *I'm in trouble, help me.* And the third, the one she'd used, means, *I'm in trouble, give me a diversion so I can handle it.*

"Yes," I said. "Yes, Miss Summerton. I have an extra instruction booklet. I'll bring it right over."

I put the phone down and stared at the wall, but there was really nothing to think about. The emergency drill gave

me no discretion. The agent in trouble calls the signals.
Of course, as her senior, it was my prerogative to disregard her call entirely and leave her to the wolves if I
thought the operation required it; but if I took action, it
had to be the type of action she'd requested.

She'd asked for a diversion, not active help. Whatever
the trouble was in there, she was going to handle it herself, all one hundred pounds of her. I thought of the smooth-
working team of Catherine and Max, and the ruthless
professional way they'd cooperated in slipping that needle
into my neck. . . .

I looked at my watch. Ten minutes should be about
right, I decided, long enough so whoever had her covered
—as somebody presumably did—would start to get tense
and nervous, but not so long that they'd know for sure
something was wrong. I spent the time sticking a few things
into my pockets that might come in handy. The low sun
hit me hard as I left my room, carrying the yellow instruction booklet that had accompanied the questionnaires.

Around the corner, the swimming pool patio was full of
half-naked kids. Some grownups lounged in long chairs by
the pool, but it was the kids who were doing the splashing
and yelling. I waited until the space around Sheila's door
was clear for a moment, and walked up quickly and ham-
mered on it hard with my fist.

"Open up!" I called as loudly as I dared. "Open up.
This is the police!"

It wasn't what you'd call really clever; in fact it was
pretty corny. Well, most diversions are. You start a fight
or set fire to a wastebasket or shoot off a gun or a firecracker. The rest is up to the other person, the person in
trouble, and he had better move fast—or she had.

I heard a sudden scuffle behind the door. A small-caliber
gun went off in there. The crack of it was unmistakable
to me, but nobody around seemed to notice, perhaps because of the kid-noises around the pool. There was a long,
long pause. I fought back the impulse to shout silly questions or break down the door. Then it opened and Sheila
looked out. She was holding a slim-barreled .22 automatic
pistol I'd never seen before.

"I had to break his finger with the trigger-guard before
he'd let go," she said calmly. "Otherwise no damage except
a hole in the ceiling. Did anybody hear the shot?"

I shook my head. I wanted to take her in my arms and

kiss her hard for being unharmed, and the hell with her little white lies. But it was hardly the time for a sentimental clinch.

"Good work, Skinny," I said, and I walked past her and looked at the stocky, baldish man sitting on the bed with a sick look on his face, nursing his hand, one finger of which stuck out at a crazy angle.

"It's Ernest Head," Sheila said unnecessarily behind me. I heard the door close. She went on: "His wife is missing. He thought we might know where she is. When I said I didn't know, he made me call you."

Looking down at the man on the bed, I had that half-smug, half-guilty feeling you get when your most diabolical schemes start to pay off.

"He knocked on the door right after I got here," Sheila was saying. "I guess I'd mentioned I was staying at this motel when I interviewed him last night. He stuck the gun in my face and forced his way in. He was talking rather wildly. He seemed to think I knew a lot of things I didn't. I could probably have disarmed him sooner, but it seemed better to let him talk."

Her voice was still quite calm. I glanced at her. There was a darkness to her eyes, a tightness to her mouth, that indicated that being closed up in a room with a wild man with a gun hadn't been quite as easy as she'd like to have me think, but it was a harmless and natural deception. Whatever had happened in Costa Verde, she'd made up for it here.

"What did he have to say?" I asked.

"His real name in Schwarzkopf, Ernst Schwarzkopf. His wife's real name is . . . was, before she married him, Gerda Landwehr." Sheila glanced at me rather accusingly. "You knew?"

"I heard the names last night, you know where."

The man on the bed looked up. "Gerda," he said. "Gertrude . . . Trudie . . . Where is she? What have you done with her?"

Sheila said, "Currently Gertrude Head is a middle-aged American housewife with dark hair. I met her last night. But once, he says, back in Germany, Gerda Landwehr was blonde and beautiful—and strictly on the make."

"She just wanted fun," Head protested. "All girls do. She wanted fun and money and music and dancing."

"They were going to be married," Sheila said. "But then

the Nazis came along, and the war, and Gerda got some better propositions and took them. She apparently had several uniformed playmates, one in particular, who got stationed in one of the camps—the same camp as a certain general we've heard of. I gather she made herself a bit conspicuous there. There was that woman who had lampshades made of human skin, remember? Gerda seems to have had a few ideas along the same lines."

"That isn't true!" Head said quickly. "I told you! It was all lies, lies, made up by people who were jealous! Gerda never—"

Sheila said, "Anyway, the war went the wrong way, and the Nazi bubble burst. One day there was a knock on Ernst's door. He opened it, and there was his glamorous Gerda, starving, half-frozen, in rags. The hounds were on her trail. She'd been on the run for months. She could run no longer. All she wanted was a place to lie down and rest, she said. She didn't expect his forgiveness. He could do as he pleased, just so he let her rest in his warm room for a moment, and gave her something to eat, before he called the authorities. You can guess the rest. He hid her out and finally, somehow, got them both to America under assumed names. They've been here ever since."

Ernest Head looked up. "We have led good, useful lives here. We have done no harm. Is there no end? Is she never to be allowed to live down a mistake made in youth, fifteen, twenty years ago? Why can't you leave her in peace?" He hesitated. "At least tell me where she is. Tell me what is happening to her. Please."

I said, "Tell me what you think is happening to her."

"I think you are interrogating her somewhere, maybe abusing her. To make her talk."

"About what?" I asked. "About something that happened in a Nazi concentration camp fifteen or twenty years ago? You have led good useful lives here, Mr. Head. So you said. You've done no harm. What would your wife have to talk about at this late date that would be of interest to anyone?"

There was a long silence. I made a slight sign to Sheila. She moved closer. Head was looking down at his hurt hand. I slipped a small case out of my pocket, which Sheila palmed. She went silently into the bathroom.

"Well, Mr. Head?" I said.

"There was a telephone call," he said without raising his

eyes. "Many months ago, almost a year. I saw Gerda's face change as she answered. The man at the other end knew everything. It was blackmail. She had to obey."

"What were the orders?"

"We often go camping in good weather. We were to drive south, into the desert, and camp there. And look for rocks. I collect rocks. A jeep came and took Gerda away. She was gone for two days. Then she came back and we returned to Tucson."

"Did she say where she'd been?"

He shook his head. "But afterwards we bought the portable radio, and she would listen to the short-wave at certain times, and sometimes she would go out or people would come to the house, people I did not know."

I said, "Is it to be the Fourth Reich, Ernest? Here on the two American continents?" He didn't answer. I asked, "How did Gerda take it? Was she happy when she came back from the two-day trip? Excited? Expectant? Triumphant maybe?"

He looked up quickly and started to speak, but checked himself. "I told you," he said sullenly. "She was forced to cooperate. She could do nothing else."

"She could have called the American authorities."

"And revealed herself?" He shuddered. "You forget, she is on the list. *They* are still after her. They will never give up. They are not human. If they learned where she was living, they would come, like vultures out of the sky." He looked at me for a moment. "Perhaps you are the ones. The ones we have been fleeing all these years. If you are, I have only one thing to ask. Make it swift. Finish it. Don't drag it out any longer. It has gone on long enough."

"Sure," I said. "Now let me look at that hand." I bent over him and took the hand and examined it. "It'll take a doctor to set the finger. But we'll give you something to kill the pain."

I had the one hand. I clamped down on the other before he could snatch it away and nodded to Sheila, who'd come up behind him. He gasped a protest, but I held him steady while she slipped the hypo into his arm. Catherine Smith and her Man Friday had no monopoly on the technique or the equipment. It's practically standard among professionals these days. Ernest Head struggled very briefly; then he sighed and went to sleep. We arranged him comfortably on the bed.

"How much did you give him?" I asked.

"The max. Four hours," Sheila said.

"We'll get somebody in to take care of him," I said. "Maybe they'll keep him at the ranch for a little, although they don't really like to use the place for that purpose. Somebody'll have to find out about his kids and make arrangements before too many questions get asked." I frowned. "Where'd you put that .22?"

"It's on the dresser."

"Bring it along. These sawed-off .38s Washington keeps wishing off on us are too damn noisy." I drew a long breath. "Well, let's go find the infamous Gerda Landwehr."

XVII

WE TOOK THE LITTLE Volkswagen because the station wagon was starting to act up again and I didn't want to wind up sitting by the roadside waiting for a mechanic. I had to run the bucket seat back to make room for my legs. Sheila got in beside me. I had a little trouble remembering where they'd hidden the reverse gear on this particular four-speed shift, but she volunteered no help. She remained silent as we drove away. When she spoke at last, her voice had a reproachful note.

"You knew?"

"That the Horst Wessel was beamed at Mrs. Head, not hubby? Let's say I guessed."

"How?"

"Head wasn't followed, remember? It was the first thing we checked. If they were trying to drive *him* into some betraying action, would they let him cruise around town unescorted?"

"Oh."

"And then," I said, "there was Catherine's exotic costume."

Sheila glanced at me quickly. "But she was obviously dressed to entertain a man, not a woman!"

"That's right," I said. "With emphasis on the obviously. Why would she go to the trouble of getting all dressed up sexy for poor old Ernest, if he were the target? She had him scared silly, she didn't need to seduce him, too. A dog whip was all she needed for Ernest. But we were butting in; she could expect a call from one of us. And we'd followed Ernest, remember? Max was undoubtedly watching. He'd have reported that we'd attached ourselves to the wrong member of the Head menage. Well, if that's whom we thought important, Catherine wasn't about to disillusion us, so she dug out her best black nylons and negligee to make it look as if she, too, were interested in a man across the way, not a woman."

"It must have been a strain for her," Sheila said dryly. "Acting as if she were interested in a man, I mean."

I said, "As long as she could keep us chasing after Ernest, she had Gerda for herself. That's the principle with which she started. I confused the issue a little by singing that pretty song with her—making myself look like a promising source of information right at hand—but once we got that misunderstanding straightened out, she returned to her original line."

"But you wouldn't tell me," Sheila said grimly. "You let me practically get heat exhaustion watching Ernest this morning, when you knew all the time—"

"It saved you the trouble of acting natural for Max's benefit," I said. "I figured he'd be checking up to see if we were taking the bait. And then I didn't know how sensitive your conscience might be."

"Conscience?" Sheila looked at me in surprise. "What's conscience got to do with it?"

I said, "You're slow this afternoon, Skinny. All that sun must have affected the brain. I threw Gerda to the blonde barracuda last night. Don't you remember? I looked her in the eye and practically told her she had one day to work on Gerda without interference. Now let's go see what kind of a job she's done."

Sheila started to speak but changed her mind. I aimed the Volkswagen towards Saguaro Heights. I had a moment of worry as we approached the place. Everything depended on whether or not the construction workers quit at noon on Saturday. If they'd been there all day, we'd have to look elsewhere, and it would be hard to know where to start. Well, it wasn't essential that we locate the scene of the crime, but it would be tidier that way.

As we approached the part of the development that was

under construction, I saw that the half-built houses were all deserted except for some kids playing on the piles of dirt thrown up by a mechanical ditch-digger. The garage in which I'd spent an unpleasant hour the night before looked different in the fading daylight, raw and new and unfinished. I parked the VW around the corner, took the .22 from Sheila, and told her what to do. Then I made my way silently around to the side door of the garage and waited for her to do it.

I heard her come running up to the big roll-up front door, laughing and breathless. Her voice reached me, high and childlike: "Hey, kids, let's see what's in this one!"

As she rattled the door handle at that end of the garage, I swung the side door open and stepped inside. It worked like a charm. Max was caught flat-footed looking the other way. I hadn't been sure he'd be here, of course, but I'd hoped for it, and he wasn't a man I wanted to walk in on without some small advantage.

He sensed my presence and turned, reaching into his shirt, but stopped when he saw Head's long-barreled .22 aimed at him.

"Easy," I said. I raised my voice. "Okay, Skinny. Everything's under control. Keep your eyes open out there."

Max was watching the gun. "The weapon isn't necessary, Mr. Evans," he said.

"The hell it isn't," I said. "I told your girl friend, if there's a doublecross all bets are off. What does this look like?"

I gestured towards the woman tied in the chair I'd had the privilege of occupying the night before. Mrs. Gertrude Head, once the belle of the Third Reich, sagged limply against her bonds, wearing only a pair of sandals and a pair of pink trousers, the kind of cheap, tight, tapering high-water pants that have taken the place of the old-fashioned housedress in which my mother used to do her cooking and cleaning. I suppose that comes under the heading of progress. Mrs. Head had obviously been caught by surprise, at home. Her dark hair was in curlers, some of which had come unwound. She was quite dead.

Well, they could hardly have turned her loose to talk. Maybe, after what had been done to her, she'd even been glad to have it come. *Make it swift,* Ernest Head had said, *finish it.* It hadn't been swift, but at least it was finished.

I thought the bone-deep brand on the forehead an unnecessary embellishment.

Max stirred. "We got the information unexpectedly. We were going to tell you as soon as—"

"Sure," I said. "Sure, you were going to tell me. As soon as you got von Sachs out of Mexico, you were going to tell me. I bet Catherine's on the road right now." His expression told me I was right. I said, "You had to wait here to take care of me—you knew I'd be along—and to get the evidence out of here; you were going to join her later. Well, don't hold your breath waiting for that happy reunion, Max."

"What are you going to do with me?"

"You have a choice," I said. "If you'll let me take your gun peacefully, I'll get some people in here who'll just hold you where you can't interfere. On the other hand, if you simply can't resist scratching that itch under your armpit, well, we can work it that way, too."

"You won't shoot." His furrowed face was scornful. "You will not dare! You are an American agent. We have done nothing against America."

"I believe there's a law on the books about murder," I said. "I'll have to check to be absolutely sure."

"Murder? Killing a Nazi slut who entered this country illegally—"

I said, "Max, you're making a mistake, friend. You'll never reach that gun."

His deep-set eyes stared at me, daring me to act. His hand moved under his shirt. I shot him accurately through the forehead, and he came down joint by joint like a marionette when you release the strings from above. The little .22 cartridge seemed to make quite a racket in the confined garage, but I doubted that outside it would have been heard very far away.

It had been heard by Sheila, of course. She was waiting for me outside. Her face was pale. "You killed him?" I nodded, and she said accusingly, "You knew you were going to, when you had me bring Head's gun along!"

I said, "It's always a possibility when you're dealing with people like Max. If it had to happen, I didn't want to arouse the neighborhood by firing off a big .38."

She licked her lips. "But they're not enemies, Eric! I mean, regardless of their methods . . . I mean, how can you justify. . . ." Her voice faltered.

"I know what you mean," I said. "And I gave the man a choice, what more could I do? He was there to stop us, or at least delay us. That's why she left him behind and went on alone."

"You don't know that!"

"He didn't deny it," I said. "And he was ready to make a sacrifice play to keep us off Catherine's trail; he wouldn't let me take him prisoner. I wasn't about to monkey with him and get myself killed. Anyway, you shouldn't be too quick to take things for granted."

"What am I taking for granted?" she demanded.

"You're thinking of Max and Catherine as agents of some earnest anti-Nazi group with an ancient grievance, like the people who got Eichmann, aren't you?"

"Grievance! That's a mild word for it! You can hardly blame them for the way they feel after—" She stopped and frowned at me. "Aren't they? She said they were."

"Catherine says a lot of things," I said. "Some of them may even be true, but we have no real proof this one is."

Sheila blurted, "That's just rationalization! You're just saying that because you shot him!"

I sighed. "Sure."

"And Gerda? I suppose she's dead, too!"

I said, "She's dead."

"You knew she would be, didn't you?"

I said, "Let's continue the argument in the car, if you don't mind. We've got things to do. We've got to make a phone call and find somebody who'll dispose of the bodies, dead and alive, without too much embarrassing publicity. I don't envy them the job. And then we've got to pick up our gear at the motel and get after Miss Smith."

I reached for Sheila's arm to guide her over the rough ground around the half-built house. She pulled away, but after we'd got into the Volkswagen she drew a long breath and looked at me.

"I'm sorry. Maybe I was . . . a little childish. It was just so unexpected."

I said, "It was real nice in the old movies where the good guys wore white hats and the bad guys wore black ones."

She smiled, but it was obvious she wasn't quite sure which color hat I ought to wear. It's a question I've sometimes wondered about myself. Presently she stopped smiling and frowned.

"But how do you expect to catch up with the woman now?" she asked worriedly. "She may have several hours' head start."

I said, "You don't have much faith in the old maestro. We know where she's going in a general way, don't we? There's only one road into Mexico she can reasonably take. And one of the nuggets of information I picked up along the border that I neglected to share with her is the fact that the international gate at Antelope Wells closes Saturday afternoon—it closed a couple of hours ago. She couldn't possibly have got into New Mexico fast enough, after working over Gerda, to catch it open. And it doesn't open again until Monday morning. By that time we'll be lying in the hills above the town watching her go by."

XVIII

IT WASN'T QUITE that cut and dried, of course; and some thirty-six hours later, watching the sunrise from a barren knoll behind Antelope Wells, New Mexico, I kind of wished I'd made the statement sound a little less definite.

There was, after all, no law saying that Catherine Smith absolutely had to go through the town below to reach the Nacimiento Mountains. I mean, there was only the one road, but like most roads it had two ends. By making a detour of several hundred miles yesterday, she could have found a place where the border was open all weekend, and then swung far down into the Mexican state of Chihuahua to approach the Nacimientos from the south. It would have involved a lot of hard driving, but it could have been done. If it had been, we could wait here forever and get nothing but a few cactus needles for our trouble.

There was an even simpler route she could have used when she found the gate closed at The Wells. It required only a pair of pliers or a fence-cutter, some knowledge of cross-country driving, and a little nerve. I mean, the international fence between the United States and Mexico runs through endless miles of uninhabited wasteland and can hardly be called impenetrable.

You can slip through on foot with little risk of being

caught; many people do. Even getting a car across the line unseen isn't prohibitively difficult. Of course you're in trouble the first time you're stopped and asked for your papers, but down in the desolate area towards which Catherine was heading, this wasn't a problem serious enough to act as a deterrent.

I guess I was betting on her accent. I was hoping that, accustomed to the well-guarded frontiers of Europe, she wouldn't realize that all that stood between her and Mexico was a few strands of lonely barbed wire. I was gambling that in any case the idea of leaving the established road to drive off across the trackless desert would be foreign to her—a lot of people, particularly women, just aren't aware of how far off the pavement an ordinary car can be made to go if you don't mind beating it up a little.

There was also the consideration that she's probably made arrangements for an eventual rendezvous with Max, based on her entering Mexico through Antelope Wells, and that she'd rather stall a few hours waiting for the gate to open than make a drastic change of plan.

This was all very logical, but it didn't help my state of mind greatly as the sun rose and the morning wore on and I watched the little town through my binoculars, waiting for a white station wagon with Arizona plates to put in an appearance, or any car driven by a well-stacked blonde. At last Sheila, who'd been catching up on her sleep in the Volkswagen, came up to join me.

"Anything yet?" she asked. I shook my head. "What if she doesn't come?" Sheila asked.

It wasn't a question I wanted to have to answer, but I tried to sound confident as I said, "Then we'll head down into Mexico and try to pick up her tracks. She's got to hit that road somewhere."

"It seems—" Sheila hesitated. "It seems like a long chance."

"It's always a long chance," I said irritably. "Would you rather have been the one who held Gerda Landwehr's arms while I used the soldering iron on her face and asked the questions? This way Catherine's done the dirty work for us. I like it that way and so, I think, will Washington. There's less chance of a kickback. And don't forget, the girl's got a cover story that'll get her into von Sachs' hideout, complete with documents. We can use that. We can use her. The problem is just catching her and maneuvering her into a position where she's got to cooperate."

"But she wants von Sachs alive."

"Sure," I said. "So what? Once we've got our hands on the general, let her try to keep him that way. I told her, any doublecross and all bets were off. Well, they're off. I can play just as crooked poker as any bleached blonde."

Sheila frowned dubiously. "Aren't you being, well, just a little Machiavellian?"

"If it works, don't knock it." I kept my voice casual. "And it's working. Here she comes."

A white station wagon was approaching down the road from the north, dragging a cloud of yellow dust behind it. I passed the binoculars to Sheila. She took a moment to adjust the focus for her eyes; then she nodded.

"I can't quite see her through the glass, but that's the car Max was following me around in. What do we do now?"

I didn't answer immediately. I reclaimed the binoculars and watched the station wagon drive on, past the trailer and shack that housed the American border man, who wasn't interested in people going south. The white car passed through the open gate and was stopped on the other side by a Mexican official in a khaki uniform. Catherine got out. The morning sun was bright on her elaborate hairdo. She was wearing her loose flowered blouse and snug white shorts. Even at the distance, the leg-display was impressive. I lowered the binoculars.

"We might as well break out the supplies and eat," I said. "The Mexican border routine takes a while; and we want to let her get well on her way before we put in an appearance down there. I'd better figure out a place to hide the rifle. I seem to recall they're kind of sensitive about firearms. . . ."

An hour later we went through the border formalities in our turn, with the .30-06 Winchester tucked inside the Volkswagen's rear-seat cushion, and various other weapons distributed about our persons, but the Mexican officials seemed to be concerned only with the engine number of the car. Once we'd located that, and paid fees for both humans and machinery, it was plain sailing, and we drove on with a little sticker on the windshield to prove we were in the country legally.

A mile or so beyond the edge of town I checked my watch, stopped the Volkswagen, and got out to examine the ground ahead. Already the road was no more than a pair of ruts running south into a flat, barren landscape of mesquite and cactus, with bluish bluffs and mesas showing around the distant horizon. I got back into the car.

"What were you looking for?" Sheila asked when we were rolling again, if you could call it that. The road didn't encourage any speed beyond a slow crawl.

"I wanted to make sure I'd recognize her tire tracks," I said. "Not that we're likely to hit enough traffic to confuse the issue. And I doubt that tracking is going to be necessary in any case." I glanced at my watch again. "She's only an hour and fifteen minutes ahead of us. We'll poke along behind, making sure the wheels don't fall off this bug. I'm betting we'll find her within fifty miles. She'll be sitting by the roadside waiting for us—well, for somebody."

"What do you mean?"

I said, "That's not the most patient girl in the world, and I don't think she's had much experience with this kind of country and this kind of driving. She's been delayed, remember. She had a head start from Tucson but she's lost it. She knows that if Max failed to stop us we'll be breathing down her neck. She may drive carefully at first, but pretty soon she'll gain confidence and start pushing. And you just don't do that out here. Sooner or later she'll hit a bump or a rock or a soft spot a little too fast. Scratch one junior-grade Ford. All we've got to watch out for is that we don't pile up this little heap, too, and put us all on foot. *And* that we don't run into any cute little ambushes and let her take it away from us."

I'd called it very close. Actually it was fifty-three miles before, leaving the VW below a rise and scouting ahead on foot, I spotted the white station wagon stuck in a sandy arroyo. I went back to the car, pulled up the rear seat, got out the rifle, and loaded it. I gave it to Sheila, who'd come around the car to watch.

"You'll cover me," I said. "She's hung up in a wash about a mile and a half ahead. I'll give you time to get into position on that little ridge to the west. Then I'll drive up dumb and innocent and let her get the drop on me. It's safer that way. If we try to surprise her, somebody might get killed."

"Safer!" Sheila's voice was concerned. "If what she wants is our car, what makes you think she won't simply shoot you?"

"She doesn't just want the car," I said. "She'll want to know what happened in Tucson after she left. She'll want to know about Max. She'll talk before she shoots. Now let's get our signals straight. Assume I'm covered, with my hands in

the air, like this. If I close the right one like this—my right
—that means you put a shot into the ground somewhere near
us to let her know you're there. If I close the left one, shoot
a leg out from under her. Under no circumstances shoot for
anything but arms or legs. We want her alive. Remember
that."

"Right, dirt. Left, leg." Sheila's face was a little pale,
but her voice was steady. "All right, Eric."

"If I drop flat, that means things are about to get really
tough, and you're supposed to open up to distract her from
me. But watch what you're doing. That .30-06 packs a respectable wallop. We don't want her dead, or me either.
Okay?"

"Okay." She looked down at the rifle in her hands. After
a moment she looked up. "Be careful, darling."

"Sure," I said. "I'll give you half an hour. On your way."

As she turned from me, I realized that maybe I'd been
supposed to kiss her or something. After all, we'd made love
and shared some fairly intimate conversation. However, I was
too busy thinking about the problem ahead to keep track of
what sentimental gestures might be expected of me. It was
kind of like going into the bush after a man-eating tigress
that, although dangerous, was worth a lot of money if it
could be delivered alive to the zoo.

I moved away from the car a reasonable distance and
settled down in the mesquite to watch. After all, Catherine
could have heard us coming. That little air-cooled engine
isn't the most silent mill in the world. She might not wait
for us to come to her.

Nothing moved in the mesquite or along the road. The
sky was clear and blue and the sun was bright and hot and
there was no sign of life on the desert. Up ahead the
saw-toothed silhouette of the Nacimientos was visible now,
low on the horizon. Behind, in the direction of Antelope
Wells, there was nothing but the endless ruts of the road in
the barren plain.

I gave Sheila the full half hour I'd promised her. Then I
got back into the Volkswagen, started it up, and drove slowly
forward along the road, such as it was. At a guess, this had
once been the main north-south Indian trail through this
region, later followed by ox-drawn Mexican *carretas* cutting
deep tracks that had been elaborated by the rubber-tired
vehicles of more modern times. When the old tracks got too
deep in a given spot, the next guy coming along had just

moved the thoroughfare off into the desert a few yards and started making new ones. In places I had a choice of three or four different routes, all terrible.

Presently I reached the edge of the arroyo. I stopped on the bank, looking at the station wagon out there. She'd really got it dug in. Coming too fast, she'd apparently been caught unawares by the sudden drop and plunged down the bank to hit the rough crossing below much too hard. She'd lost control and swerved out into the soft sand. Trying to back out, she'd buried the rear wheels to the hubcaps.

There was nobody in the station wagon. Nothing moved in the low brush along the bank. I got out of the VW, taking the keys with me. I walked down the bank and across the sand to the white car. There was chewed-up brush around the rear wheels where she'd tried to get traction and failed. I bent over to pick up a handful of sand at the rear of the wagon. It smelled strongly of gasoline. She'd not only managed to get herself stuck, she'd apparently put a rock through the gas tank as well.

Still bending, in the most helpless and tempting position possible, I heard her rise from the mesquite on the bank above and behind me.

"When you straighten up, Mr. Evans," she said, "I want to see your hands above your head. Don't turn until I tell you."

XIX

STANDING MOTIONLESS with my hands in the air, I heard Catherine jump lightly from the bank and come across the sand towards me. She undoubtedly had a gun, probably the little automatic pistol I'd seen before, but it didn't really worry me, not yet. Even if she wasn't a very good back-road driver, she was still a pro. Her gun wouldn't go off until she wanted it to go off.

I was actually more uneasy over the fact that Sheila—by this time established some hundred-odd yards away on the ridge, I hoped—was presumably watching for my signal through the telescopic sight, which meant that the damn rifle was aimed straight at me. I still wasn't quite sure about Sheila. I hoped she wouldn't get nervous or careless out there.

"All right," Catherine said behind me. "Turn around slowly, Mr. Evans. Very slowly and carefully."

I turned and looked at the little automatic in her hand. I noted that her hand was dirty. In fact, the whole girl looked kind of generally mussed and sweaty from working on her car and waiting in the mesquite under the hot desert sun.

I said, "You're a lousy driver, honey. Just because there are ruts doesn't mean you have to drive in them, you know. That's a differential housing between the rear wheels, not a plow. I could have tracked you from Antelope Wells by the furrow you cut down the high center of the road."

"Road!" she said indignantly. "You call this a road? I am a very good driver on a real road, but this obstacle course . . .! I thought you said it was in good shape."

"I did say that, didn't I?" I grinned. "Just like you said Ernest Head was the man with the information we wanted."

After a moment she smiled faintly. "I see. So you were being clever also."

"I'm a very clever guy," I said. "Good with a gun, too. Max sends his regards, honey. From hell."

It was meant to shake her and it did. She stared at me, and there was sudden murder in her blue eyes. Her grubby hand even tightened a bit on the little pistol—all except the trigger finger. After several seconds she let her breath go out softly.

"So? What happened?"

I said, "He was careless or tired; he let me get the drop on him. And then, well, he must have been reading some of this quick-draw bunk. He thought he could outdraw a gun that was already covering him. Or, silly boy, he thought I wouldn't shoot."

"I was fond of Max," she murmured. "You run a big risk telling me this."

I shook my head. "No. It would have been a bigger risk not telling you. I don't know what your arrangements were, but as long as you could hope for other help eventually, you could afford to shoot me. But without Max you need me. You can't possibly take von Sachs alone unless you're willing to take him dead and die doing it. I don't think you're that much of a fanatic. If you're going to get out alive, you'll need assistance. So you might as well tell me: what did you and Max get out of Gerda Landwehr about the location of our general's hideout?"

She laughed shortly. "You don't really think I'll tell you that!"

"I really think so," I said.

"You are at my mercy," she said.

"Let's not talk utter nonsense," I said. "You haven't got any mercy for me to be at. And you're covered from behind by a heavy-caliber rifle."

There was a little silence. A wry smile touched Catherine's lips briefly. "I see," she murmured. "I see. That is very good. You have restored my faith in you, Mr. Evans. I thought you walked into the trap just a little too readily. So you did not come down here into Mexico alone? The little girl is behind me?"

"Yes. Up on that ridge to the west."

"Prove it to me."

"Sure." I closed my right hand, still raised, into a fist. There was a moment's pause, long enough for doubt to go through my mind; then sand sprayed up suddenly a few yards away from us and the sound of the rifle reached us, flat and hard. "Okay?" I said to Catherine.

"Okay," she said. She grimaced and put her pistol away inside her blouse. "Well, that throws an altogether different light on the situation, doesn't it? I accept your offer of assistance, Mr. Evans. I can certainly use the help of a man who is clever and good with a gun. The place we want, according to Gerda Landwehr, is known as the Caves of Copala. . . ."

When Sheila reached us, she seemed shocked to find us sitting on the bank side by side with our legs dangling, talking like old friends. She was really a rather naive and inexperienced little girl. She apparently still believed in things like love and hate and gratitude and vengeance, not realizing that they had no place in this work, where your enemy one minute is your ally the next—and maybe your enemy again a few minutes later. I wasn't forgetting that possibility, of course.

Sheila stopped in front of us, flushed from the sun, with the Winchester slung over one shoulder. I reminded myself that whether she knew it or not I owed her an apology for the doubts I'd had about her. Whatever had happened in El Fuerte's hut in Costa Verde, she'd handled Ernest Head beautifully in Tucson, and she'd been right on the job here.

But this wasn't the time to set the record straight. I just grinned at her approvingly.

"Good show, Skinny, as the British say," I told her. "Sit down. I want you to hear this, too."

Catherine was drawing pictures in the dirt. "We've come about fifty miles already," she said. "We turn off about twenty miles ahead. The Landwehr woman wasn't too sure about the exact distances, but she gave me a landmark, a red butte. From there we climb some forty miles back into the Nacimientos. Copala Canyon runs east and west. It is deep and very narrow for a couple of miles from the entrance. Then it widens and there are many old cliff dwellings in the south wall. Von Sachs is pretending to investigate them scientifically: the Caves of Copala. Actually he is gathering a force of armed men there." Catherine looked up. "Now you can shoot me. I have told you all I know. You do not need me any longer."

I said, "We need you to get in there."

She was smiling. "Yes, there is that, is there not? I will get my things out of my car."

We watched her move away across the sand. Her white shorts were smudged behind. It didn't make her walk look any less provocative. I heard Sheila make an indignant little sound.

"Relax, Skinny," I said. "You did swell. Let's not get temperamental now, huh?"

"I was hoping you'd signal with your left hand," Sheila whispered fiercely. "I can't stand her. I'd just love to shoot her."

"Sure. Don't give up hope. The job isn't over yet."

We had a little trouble getting the Volkswagen across the wash, and we had more trouble further on, as the road left the open desert and started winding through great slanting fields of broken rock that sloped up to the west into the Nacimiento foothills. We didn't reach Gerda Landwehr's red butte until well past noon.

Ironically, after the trouble we'd had to find it, the trail into the mountains was unmistakable. Apparently somebody, either von Sachs or some Mexican mining or ranching outfit, had brought in some heavy equipment from the south, which was now the direction of the nearest real road going anywhere. You couldn't miss where the big truck tires had swung westward. The wind had erased the pattern of the treads, but the depressions remained, leading back into the hills.

From there it was uphill work, with the little Volkswagen engine screaming in the low gears hour after hour, steadily, except for an occasional stop to roll a boulder out of the way or find a passable route around an immovable obstacle. The afternoon was well along when we finally came within sight of the mouth of Copala Canyon. It was a narrow cleft in a cliff of funny-looking rock that seemed to be pock-marked with holes. I didn't know enough geology to tell whether they were the gas pockets of an old lava flow or the results of later erosion, and it didn't really matter. What counted was that there'd be plenty of caves in the stuff big enough for prehistoric Indians to have lived in, which seemed to confirm Catherine's story.

I stopped the car where the tracks started across an open valley towards the cliff. I got out and put my glasses on the entrance. No guards or sentries were visible but that didn't mean they weren't there. I pulled the car door wide and spoke to Sheila, in the cramped rear seat. Ostensibly she'd been put there because she was the smallest; actually I'd preferred not to have Catherine sitting behind me where I couldn't see her.

"Okay, doll," I said to Sheila. "We'll take the rifle and ammo, the canteen, and a couple of those big chocolate bars. Also, we've got to get all our personal belongings out of this heap. We'll cache them somewhere. Catherine doesn't want anything aboard to indicate that she didn't come alone."

Sheila's small face had a rebellious look, but she'd already made her argument against the plan and been overruled; she decided against further protests. Catherine came around to help, and shortly we had the gear in a pile by the roadside. I took the car keys from my pocket, regarded the blonde girl for a moment, and dropped them into her hand.

"It's all yours," I said.

"I appreciate your trust," she said, smiling faintly.

"Trust, hell," I said. "Sheila and I have enough food and water here to make civilization on foot without your help, but once you're in that rat-trap you'll never get out without us, car or no car. Who's trusting whom?"

She didn't answer. She looked hot and wilted and dusty like the rest of us: it had been a long, rough ride. I reached out and deliberately yanked off the topmost button of her blouse and threw it away.

"That improves the view," I said, eyeing her judiciously. "A little brassiere show never hurts. As I recall his record, von Sachs isn't exactly a monk."

Catherine said dryly, "There's a saying: teach your grandmother to suck eggs. I never really understood it, but I believe it's appropriate here, Mr. Evans."

"Sure. You're a genius and you don't need any advice, but don't forget to muss up your hair some more before you get there. Smear a little dirt on your face, maybe. You're an Argentine Nazi and you've gone through terrible hardships to reach von Sachs and warn him of danger, remember?"

"I'll remember." Her voice was cool.

"I'll be along presently to play the supporting role," I said. "There's no use trying to write the dialogue in advance. We've covered the main points. The rest we'll have to improvise and hope for the best."

"Just so you come," she said, watching me closely.

"You'd be in kind of a spot if I didn't, wouldn't you?" I grinned. "Well, that's the chance you take, honey. Once I'm in, I'll be depending on you, so it comes out even." I hesitated. There are times when deceit is necessary, but there are also times when a certain amount of honesty, judiciously applied, can create a valuable atmosphere of confidence in the midst of suspicion. I said, "Before you start, let's put all the cards on the table. You know damn well we can't get him out of that hole alive, don't you? Not if he's got as many men in there as Mrs. Head indicated. We're going to have trouble enough getting ourselves out afterward, so let's not kid around any more about taking von Sachs anywhere for trial. It just isn't practical."

Catherine was silent for a second or two. Then she sighed and said relucantly, "You are right, of course. Just so I can report him dead, that will have to be enough. I will have to disregard my instructions to that extent. I am permitted a certain amount of discretion. Well, I had better go."

"*Hasta la vista,* as we say in this part of the country."

"And *auf Widersehen* to you, Mr. Evans."

She got into the car and drove off without looking back. I couldn't help thinking that she'd yielded her point of principle a little too easily. I didn't kid myself for a moment that I knew everything that went on in her mind. Standing there, watching the VW making its bouncy way across the valley towards the opening in the pockmarked cliff, I felt Sheila come up beside me. She'd been waiting a little distance off,

obviously dissociating herself from the whole affair. I turned
to look at her.

"You still no like, eh?"

She said, "It's an absolutely crazy plan! You know you
can't trust her!"

I didn't like doing it, but it was no time for personal
differences. I said deliberately, "She's a pro. I can trust her
to act like a pro, not like a sentimental kid full of likes and
dislikes that have nothing to do with the job at hand. You're
out of line, Skinny."

Sheila's face got quite pale. "I'm sorry," she whispered.
"I'm sorry you think my attitude is unprofessional, and I
certainly didn't mean to intrude my childish opinions . . . !"
She stopped and turned abruptly away. After a moment she
asked in a choked voice, "Where do you want to hide all
this stuff?"

We hauled our luggage some distance off the trail and
concealed it in a mess of brush and boulders after first
making sure we weren't disturbing any rattlesnakes at their
afternoon siestas. It looked like that kind of a place. Then,
with the rifle and supplies, we hunted up a place where we
could climb to the top of the cliff, unseen from the entrance
to the canyon. The purpose of the operation was, if possible,
to establish a marksman on the canyon rim above von Sachs'
camp: an outside man—or girl—to support the two inside
agents at the critical moment.

The approach reminded me, somehow, of Costa Verde.
There was the hostile company, the danger ahead, the rifle
banging my back as I climbed and hiked, and the wild, unfamiliar landscape. I found that my leg was giving me much
less trouble; otherwise, the only real difference was in the
humidity, and in the fact that instead of being accompanied
by a score of trained fighting men, I had with me only one
small, resentful girl.

"Well, that should be about it," I said at last, stopping
to catch my breath. "If Gerda Landwehr's dope was correct,
and Catherine transmitted it accurately, and the damn canyon doesn't wiggle around too much, we should be just
about opposite those cliff dwellings. The canyon edge should
be right up ahead. Wait here." I glanced at her. "Go easy
on that water. It's all we have."

She gave me a look of annoyance, capped the canteen,
and moved over to sit sulkily in the shade of a rock. Well,
I hadn't come down into Mexico for love and affection. I

moved ahead slowly toward where the canyon ought to be if I hadn't lost my bearings completely during the climb. One moment I was looking at what seemed to be just a continuous rocky mountainside, but when I took another step forward, the ground opened up practically at my feet.

I got down and crawled to the canyon edge and looked at the Caves of Copala as a hostile Indian scout might have, centuries before. But it wasn't the caves across the way that caught my attention first. It was the thing standing in the cottonwood grove upstream with a camouflage net over it to hide it from aerial observation: a thing that looked like a gigantic .300 Magnum cartridge.

I'd been wondering just what kind of heavy equipment von Sachs had been dragging up into his mountain stronghold. Now I knew.

XX

THERE WAS A SCUFFLING sound as Sheila crawled up beside me. She was silent for quite a long interval. When she spoke, the antagonism was completely gone from her voice, as if she'd realized at last that this was no time for personal grievances.

"What is it?" she whispered.

"You should know," I said. "You're the one who spotted it for us in the first place."

"Oh," she said. "That thing. I just saw it come through the village on a trailer. I never saw it set up. But that was over a thousand miles south. How did they get it *here*?"

"That," I said, "is a damn good question."

I studied the scene below. The caverns across the way had been elaborated by ancient masons working with rocks and mud mortar until they formed a kind of apartment complex in the face of the canyon wall, reached by crude wooden ladders. Men were obviously living up there now, perhaps for the first time in centuries. Below the cave dwellings, out in the open, was a tent, a campfire, a few men, a couple of pickup trucks, and a blue Volkswagen sedan. There was no sign of a blonde woman in shorts, and at the moment I wasn't interested except to note that she'd made it. At least the car had.

All the stuff in the clearing looked innocent enough for a scientific expedition. A plane flying over would spot nothing out of the ordinary. But there was the missile concealed among the trees upstream; and downstream, before the canyon narrowed again, in another bunch of cottonwoods, was a mass of vehicles disguised by matte camouflage paint. I could make out some vintage jeeps and six-by-six Army trucks, apparently old war-surplus stuff picked up somewhere at a bargain. Down there, also, was the chunky six-wheeled trailer that hauled and controlled the missile, with its antennas and oversized cab.

It wasn't very impressive, aside from the bird. Say at most a couple of hundred armed men and enough vehicles to transport them as far as the beat-up equipment could be made to run. Say, up in the States, small welcoming committees of people like those we'd investigated in Tucson: a surly unemployed mechanic who liked his beer, a knife-packing young *pachuco*, the fading former mistress of a former Nazi butcher-boy. On the face of it, always discounting the bird, you could hardly call it a menacing display of power.

But there was always the bird—and not only the bird but the fact that they'd got it here. There must have been a ship involved, a difficult embarkation and landing, and countless impossible miles at night over back roads and no roads at all, always under threat of discovery. Guile and bluff and incredible labor were represented by that missile standing in the cottonwoods. People who could accomplish that weren't to be dismissed easily.

"In case they didn't tell you in Washington or you weren't in condition to listen closely," I said, "it's a misplaced Russian toy known as the Rudovic III. It has a nuclear warhead and a twelve-hundred-mile range. That gives it a choice, from here, of any big U.S. city from Los Angeles, California, to Houston, Texas. Maybe farther. My geography is a little sketchy. And controlling this pleasant gadget is our scar-faced ex-Nazi general, with his pocket-sized army and his dreams of greatness, past and future."

"Did you know you were going to find it here?"

"No," I admitted. "Costa Verde reported it missing, but we didn't know whether to believe the report or not. President Avila might have hid it out for his own use and lied about it. I confess I didn't think of the possibility that von Sachs could have grabbed it."

"I suppose—" Sheila hesitated. "I suppose we have to do something about it."

I grimaced. "Well, we could just pop Heinrich from up here and beat it, leaving Catherine to the wolves and the firecracker to whoever wants it. It's a real temptation, now that I look at the setup. I didn't know it was going to be this pretty, like a target range, when I agreed to join our blonde friend inside."

Sheila said in a tentative voice, "Catherine would desert us in an instant if she saw anything to be gained by it."

"I know," I said. "It's just that damn Roman candle that keeps me honest. I caught hell for leaving it once, way down in Central America. This close to the U.S. I've got no choice. I've got to put it out of commission somehow, before some irresponsible jerk down there goes and pushes the wrong button. Come on, let's move back a bit, and get the operation lined up."

In the shade of a boulder well back from the rim I took a sparing drink from the canteen and slipped the rifle off. The leather sling hadn't done my burns any good, and I couldn't help remembering who'd given them to me. It wouldn't really have hurt my conscience greatly to leave Catherine down there in the hands of von Sachs. It was just as well, I guess, that I no longer had a choice.

I pulled the bolt out of the gun, checked the barrel, shoved five shells into the magazine, loaded one into the chamber, and handed the weapon to Sheila along with two boxes of ammunition.

"There you are, Skinny," I said. "You have forty rounds to play with. Well, you fired one back up the road. Thirty-nine."

She said, "Eric—"

I said, "The range is point-blank about two thirds of the way across the canyon, but you can't reach the tent or the campfire with hundred per cent accuracy so don't try. You know the man; you've studied the photographs. No matter what happens—I repeat, no matter what happens —don't fire a shot until you can take care of him with absolute certainty. That's your job. Once he's down and you're sure of him, you're on your own. But I'm counting on you to take out von Sachs the minute he wanders close enough. I'll steer him within range if I can. Or Catherine will. It depends on how things work out down there."

"And how are you going to—"

"Never mind me, for the moment. After you've made the touch, after von Sachs is taken care of, you can use the rest of the ammo as the spirit moves you. Cover us as well as you can, but don't hang around too long. Get out before you're cut off up here. If we make it clear, we'll be waiting for you below, where we cached the suitcases. With a car if we can manage."

"And—" She paused. "And if you're not there?"

"Don't wait around for us," I said. "You've got most of a gallon of water and enough nourishment to keep you going. Walk due east until you hit the Antelope Wells road, but don't try to get back up to the border, it's much too far. Turn south when you reach the road. There are some little Mexican towns farther down. Or somebody'll come along and give you a lift. Just make sure they're okay before you let them see you. It'll be a long, hot, dusty hike, it may take several days even, but you can make it if you go easy on the water."

She gave a funny little laugh. "You're being awfully silly. Do you really think I'd go off without you. I'm not Catherine, you know."

I said evenly, "The standing orders expressly forbid an agent's risking his life to rescue the captured, succor the wounded, or bury the dead, unless the success of the mission is involved. Here it won't be. We'll either get our work done in the first few minutes after the action starts, or we won't. You've got farther to go than we have, over rougher terrain. If we're not waiting at the cache by the time you reach it, we're just not coming, that's all. Being a heroine will get you nothing. Just keep on going." I rose and glanced at my watch. "Well, I'd better start back. I don't want to have to scramble down that cliff in the dark. This would be a hell of a time to break a leg."

"Eric."

"Yes?"

Sheila leaned the gun against the boulder and rose to face me. "Be careful," she said, looking up. "Please be careful, darling. And if you say 'sure' again, the way you did the last time we separated, up the road, I'll slap your face."

I looked down at her for a moment. Her short hair was tousled, her shirt and pants were dusty, and her small face was pink from the sun: she looked like a kid after an active summer picnic.

I grinned at her. "Sure," I said. "I'll be careful, Skinny. Sure."

She made a face and brought her hand up threateningly. I caught her by the wrist. It was a mistake, touching her. I'd been trying very hard to keep everything on a business basis, to think of her simply as one of the human resources with which I had to accomplish a certain task.

That I'd once found her helpless in the jungle, that I'd carried her, cared for her, and later stuck my neck out for her officially, and made love to her unofficially, was strictly beside the point down here. Or so I tried to tell myself, but suddenly I found myself holding her and kissing her possessively, which was a hell of a way for an agent to behave within sight of the target.

"For God's sake!" I said at last, rather breathlessly. "What a hell of a time for necking. We'd better cut it out before I forget all about important things like homicide and sabotage."

She held onto me as I tried to step back. "Would that be so bad?" She was smiling mischievously. "You wouldn't have to forget very long. Just a few minutes."

"You're a shameless wench," I said.

"You told me that before."

"I don't go for women in pants. They don't do a thing for me," I said firmly. At least I hoped it was firmly. "And I've got to get down that damn cliff before dark. I've got a date with a blonde."

"I know." She grimaced. "You! Tearing a button off her blouse so you could admire her breasts. Who did you think you were fooling?"

I said, "Oh, is *that* what was eating you?"

"Yes, I'm jealous," she breathed. "She makes me feel plain and scrawny. I know it's stupid, but I can't help it. Eric."

"Yes?"

"You will be there, won't you? At the cache."

"I'm sure as hell going to try," I said.

"And afterward—"

"It's considered bad luck to make plans for afterward, Skinny."

"I know. Just so you're there. And just so you don't think—" She stopped, looking down.

"Think what?"

"That I'm just a silly little girl with a transference who's got to be humored because she's had a tough time. I'm in good health now, darling, my mind is perfectly clear, and I know what I want. What I want for us. You can be remembering that, down there with your predatory blonde. And—" She hesitated and looked up quickly. "And don't worry. I know what you've been thinking about me. Some day I'll tell you what really happened in Costa Verde. But it's all right now. I'm all right. Just get von Sachs within two hundred yards of me and I'll do the job so you'll have no complaints. You'll see."

XXI

EVERYTHING WENT ACCORDING to plan. They'd been warned by Catherine that I'd be along, they were waiting, and they caught me with the goods as they were supposed to. I had a sketch of the canyon showing the positions of the missile and control truck that wasn't half bad for the poor light in which I'd had to work. I had a list of the camouflaged vehicles parked under the trees, and an estimate of the number of men in the caves, and notes on everything else a bright intelligence type might want to bring home to his superiors to show he was on the ball. I was sorry I hadn't brought a camera and flashgun, but perhaps that would have been overdoing it.

They let me finish and closed in on me as I was trying to sneak away down the canyon. Making a run for it, I tripped and knocked my wind out, so it was easy for them— and for me, too; easier than taking a chance on a lot of excitable Latin marksmen in the dark. They might accidentally have hit me. Even worse, they might have missed me and let me get away.

They pushed me around a bit and got my notebook and the .38 revolver I'd worn for them to find. That made them happy. They'd captured a dangerous man, the man they'd been told to watch for. They marched me triumphantly back up the canyon past the vehicle park and across the little creek, a trickle now, that could be a torrent at times judging by the width of the wash and the height of the bank it had cut in places.

I didn't look up at the cliff to the north. It had long since become too dark for accurate shooting, but Sheila was probably watching nevertheless. Out here in the open, I could see my half-dozen captors more clearly. They weren't the innocent-looking, dumb-looking, lazy-looking laborers who'd been loafing around the fire for show—and still were. They were tough, dark-faced men like Jiminez' bunch in Costa Verde. Don't think I underestimated them because they'd fallen for my super-spy act. These were men, as Mexican history showed, who could march and fight forever on a handful of beans and a little chili.

They carried a variety of firearms, ranging from old Springfields and M-1's to the latest in machine pistols, one specimen, belonging to the sergeant in charge of the patrol, a small, wiry character. They were not strictly speaking in uniform; but each man had a swastika armband and a machete, although this wasn't country where a brush-knife was essential. I noticed that all the machetes were the same pattern, a little more elaborate than the usual crude, heavy blade with a couple of pieces of wood riveted on for a handle. A rudimentary brass guard had been added, like that of a saber, curving around to protect the fingers, making a fighting weapon of a wood-chopping tool.

Well, the Nazis had always believed in the psychological value of special cutlery, generally some kind of a sneaky dirk that wasn't much good for real fighting but was a hell of a fine weapon for stabbing a man in the back. Symbolically, you might say, the honest machete was a step upward, although one might be hard put to find a use for it in atomic warfare.

They took me to the wall tent set up at the base of the cliff. Now, at night, the pretense of this being a scientific expedition had been abandoned, and an armed sentry stood in front. He gave the straight-armed Nazi salute. The sergeant with the machine pistol replied in kind.

"Viva Quintana!" said the sentry.

"Viva Quintana!" said my escort, and I was shoved into the tent.

Inside, there was a square table and some folding wooden chairs. A camp cot was shoved back against the canvas wall. A two-burner gasoline lantern hung above the table, casting a harsh white light over everything.

Von Sachs sat at the table with some papers before him, facing the door sternly, like General Grant awaiting the latest word from Vicksburg. At close range he looked older than I'd expected, but brown and lean and hard. He was in khakis, with an armband. A Sam Browne belt with a .45 Colt automatic and a fancier version of the regimental machete hung from the back of his chair. A germ of an idea came to me as I looked from the saber-like weapon to the scarred face of von Sachs, and I shoved it back into the corner of my mind, hoping it would grow into a real brainwave.

Over to one side, I was aware, was Catherine Smith, but it wasn't my business to notice her until I was given a cue. In my terrible predicament I'd hardly be giving attention to stray blondes. I kept my eyes on the men.

They went through the viva-Quintana drill, and the little sergeant slapped my gun and notebook on the table and made his report in Spanish. Von Sachs picked up the notebook and glanced at my notes and drawings. He picked up my gun and checked the loads. He aimed it at me, dismissed the sergeant, and waited until the tent flaps had settled back into place before he spoke.

"Is this the man, Fräulein Schmidt?"

It was my cue and I looked. She was lounging on a camp chair drinking Mexican beer out of the bottle. You couldn't help being conscious, if you were a man, of the strong, bare, sunburned legs and the carelessly half-open blouse. She took another swig and frowned at me.

"Well, he's tall enough," she said to von Sachs. "I told you, that's all I know, that it was done by a very tall man who first represented himself as an interviewer of some kind and then said he was a U.S. government agent. He took the Head woman to the garage where I found her, forced the information from her, and left her tied. She lived just long enough to tell me this, and how to find you and warn you, before she died."

It was the story we'd more or less agreed upon while we were driving. Von Sachs was watching her closely as she talked. He seemed particularly interested in the broken threads left by the missing button of her blouse—well, that general area.

"I could think of worse places to die, Fräulein," he murmured. Then his glance sharpened suspiciously. "Gerda Landwehr only came here once. She was blindfolded at the mouth of the canyon. How could she tell you where to come?"

"She must have peeked," Catherine said without hesitation. "She described the caves. She told me what road and how far. If you don't believe she knew, ask him," she said with a gesture in my direction. "After all, he found his way here, too."

Von Sachs didn't turn at once. He seemed to be still brooding over that missing button. I suppose I might have been able to jump him while his attention was diverted, turn the gun on him, and do the job right there. Maybe we could then have shot our way clear with his gun and mine, and hers if she still had it, and got away in the dark. Maybe. The project had suicidal overtones, and I don't like switching plans. Besides, it didn't take care of the missile. Besides, I wasn't at all sure he was as absent-minded as he looked. He could have been trying to trick me into a move.

"It is too bad," he said slowly. "She was a handsome woman even after so many years—Gerda. As a girl, she was beautiful. She was the, er, fiancée of one of my junior officers, but rank has its privileges, ha! And you killed her!" he said, swinging abruptly to face me over the short-barreled revolver.

"I interrogated her," I lied. "She was soft, like all you Nazis. Soft and yellow inside. Like butter, von Sachs."

"Here I am Kurt Quintana," he snapped. "You will address me so."

"You are Kurt Quintana calling a lady Fräulein?" I sneered. "You might at least keep the act consistent. Señorita is the local word."

He frowned. "You are trying to make me angry. Why?"

"It's an old trick in these parts, von Sachs. When the Apaches caught you, you tried to make them kill you fast. It didn't hurt so much that way. Well, you've got me. Let's stop the yakking and get it over with." I grinned at him maliciously, as if remembering something. "You look a lot more dignified than the last time I saw you."

"Where was that?" he demanded suspiciously. "I do not recall—"

"You didn't see me," I said. "You were trying to get under a jeep. The first half went in fine, but the rump end kind of got left outside. It was a real tempting target. I've always regretted passing it up."

"That was you? With the rifle, in Costa Verde?"

"That was me. And let me tell you, I caught hell for letting you go. For punishment, they gave me the job of catching you again." I shrugged. "Well, it just shows you, never pass up a good shot. If I'd got you in the tail, you might have got blood poisoning and died, and we wouldn't be having this pleasant conference."

"You are an American intelligence agent?"

"I'm an American agent. If I had any intelligence of any kind I wouldn't be here, caught by a bunch of toy soldiers."

"You are alone?"

"I'm working alone. I don't say there aren't others assigned to the job of finding you, but I guess I beat them to you. I wanted to check what that woman told me before I called out the reserves. Information obtained by those methods, as you probably know, isn't always reliable." I grimaced. "Well, come on, you ersatz Fuehrer! Whistle up your firing squad. Break out that final lousy cigarette. Let's put the goddamn show on the road, huh?"

"You think I am going to kill you?"

"You're either going to kill me or tease me to death. What's the difference?"

"What is your name?"

"None of your damn business," I said. "Well, call me Evans. Henry Evans."

He looked at me for a second or two in silence. Then he lifted my snub-nosed weapon and took careful aim. The hammer started to rise, actuated by the double-action mechanism, as he put pressure on the trigger. When it got to a certain point it would fall. There was a little sound to the right as Catherine pried the top off another beer bottle.

"God, I'm dry," she said. "This country just bakes it out of you. If you're going to shoot, dearie, shoot. Don't make me wait all day for the noise."

He didn't look at her, but that didn't mean he hadn't been testing her, to see if perhaps there was something between us that might make her plead for my life. But he was watching me. The angle of the light made the scar a deep cleft in his cheek. He'd come a long way from those innocent boyish games at Heidelberg. He'd commanded armies; he'd been hunted for crimes against humanity. Now he was in command again, after a fashion. He was on his way back up, unless something stopped him.

I cleared my throat and said, "Don't keep the lady waiting, von Sachs."

He eased the pressure on the trigger and laughed. "You are frightened, Mr. Evans."

"Guns always scare me. But I'll get over it. There's very little a bullet won't cure, I always say."

"No," he said slowly, "you are frightened inside. You talk big, but it is you who are soft and yellow inside, Mr. Evans. You are afraid if I do not kill you at once, you will break down and show it."

I said, "Christ! An amateur psychologist I've got to run into, yet! Tell me one thing, von Sachs. Just what the hell were you doing with a bunch of Commies down in Costa Verde?"

"That is a foolish question," he said. "You have seen the result of my trip outside, you have sketched it in your little notebook. I was shopping for a weapon I'd been told was for sale."

I said, "Hell, El Fuerte wouldn't have sold it while he was alive. That was his ace in the hole."

"The ace was about to be trumped," von Sachs said. "His Russian backers had got wind of the fact that he had it, through informants in Cuba. They were displeased. They threatened him with dire consequences if he should use it. They wanted it back. All the time, of course, he was denying that he had ever seen such a thing. Meanwhile he was trying to find a buyer with cash. The Russians would have paid him nothing, and General Santos had gone to considerable expense and trouble. He thought it only fair that the transaction should show a profit."

"I see," I said. "And now you've got it here, how the hell are you planning to use it? I mean, you're not crazy enough to think you can blackmail either the United States or Mexico with just one overgrown whiz-bang?"

"Blackmail?" He frowned at the word. "I do not blackmail, Mr. Evans. When the time comes, not too far distant, I will fire the missile. And the city of El Paso, Texas, will disappear from the map of America. I think it will be El Paso. The bearded technicians tell me it is the easiest target within range, and your Texans are hot-headed and politically influential. They will insist on immediate retaliation—and against whom will they want to retaliate, Mr. Evans?"

I drew a long breath. "It's a tricky idea. Not original, but tricky. It might work in the movies."

"It will work here! No one up there above the border will know from which direction the missile came. All they will know is that an American city has been destroyed. Will you tell me that not one of your intercontinental weapons will be fired under such provocation? That no signal will go out to the captains of the atomic submarines with their Polaris missiles? And if one, just one, weapon is fired, will it not be answered?" He laid the gun gently on the table. "And when the radioactive dust settles, will there not be opportunities for a man at the head of a military force, with secret allies in your principal southwestern cities, Mr. Evans? Such a man could carve an empire out of the rubble!"

There was a little silence. As I'd said, the idea wasn't exactly original. Other people had thought of the possibility before, but none had gone shopping for the means to carry it out. At least I hoped they hadn't.

I said lightly, "Well, it sounds kind of like burning down the barn to roast the cow to get some bones to throw to the pup that hasn't been whelped yet. Do you know what I think? I think you're cracked, von Sachs. I think you just want to set the world on fire and watch the pretty mushroom clouds grow and grow. I think—"

"That's enough!" He had picked up the gun again.

"I think you'd just like getting the two largest countries that crushed Adolf Hitler to destroy each other. The rest is just crap for the suckers outside. Empire, hell!"

"Silence!" The hammer started to rise again.

"Go on," I said bravely. "Pull the damn trigger, you crazy Nazi butcher! Go on, shoot!"

The hammer subsided slowly. He sighed. "You are too eager to die, Mr. Evans. I do not think I will oblige you tonight. Tomorrow, perhaps. . . . Guards!"

Well, if I hadn't egged him on, if I hadn't made him think I yearned for a quick death, he'd have had me shot right away. It was very ingenious of me, and I was sweating very convincingly as they took me out of there.

XXII

THE JAIL, brig, detention cell, or what have you, was a pigeonhole twenty feet up the face of the canyon wall, reached by a rickety ladder. The sergeant made me climb up, covered by his ugly little weapon; then he sent a man up to tie me securely. The knot-man was good, and I'm no Houdini. I tried to get some slack the way it says in the manual, but if I'd thought the man could read at all, let alone read English, I'd have said he'd been at the same book. When he left me it was fairly obvious that I wasn't going to be climbing down any ladders without help. Then they took the ladder away, and that was that.

Down below, the fire was blazing cheerfully and the boys around it were passing the tequila, mescal, pulque, tiswin, or whatever kind of cactus juice it was they had in the jug. Pretty soon one of them broke out a guitar and began to sing, just like in a movie. I wiggled forward to where I could look at the happy group below. Off to one side sat a lone, anti-social character with his back to a rock and a rifle across his knees, watching my cave. The light was still burning in the tent, I noticed, and the sentry still stood in front.

The guard with the rifle waved me back. When I didn't move at once he aimed his weapon my way. I took the hint and squirmed back into the darkness of the cave and tried the other end. Ten feet back from the entrance I hit solid rock. Well, I hadn't been about to explore any tunnels or crevices tied hand and foot. It was up to Catherine now.

Her next move was obvious, and soon I could hear her working on it. Her laughter and von Sachs' began to come from the tent more loudly and drunkenly as the night progressed. Presently they started singing the Horst Wessel off key. After that there was more laughter, and some horse-play that shook the tent canvas, and a male voice demanding and a female voice protesting, not very convincingly, and some more activity, and silence.

I lay in my pigeonhole above and wondered why I didn't

like myself very much. I mean, it wasn't as if the woman were anything to me; and she'd merely done just what I would have told her to do if she'd asked for instructions.

The guitarist was long silent, and the fire was dying. When it no longer cast a glow on the ceiling of the cave, she came. I heard her down there, speaking to the guard in a slurred voice and giggling in an inebriated way at his answer; then there was a solid, whacking sound like an axe going into soft pine.

I heard the ladder being moved back into place. Something metallic was tossed into the cave. A moment later she followed it, sat for a moment panting, and crawled over to cut me free with the machete she'd sent ahead, presumably taken from the guard below.

"So!" she breathed, helping me sit up. "Now we must get down, before someone notices the ladder."

"Give me a chance to get some circulation back. What about the sentry by the tent?"

"Asleep. I was friendly. I gave him a beer. With something in it I happened to have along. Like von Sachs. They will sleep until morning, both of them. Your guard would not take a beer, a dutiful man. So he is dead. When they find him, we are betrayed. Now come. I will go first and hold you if you slip. Never mind the big knife."

"I want it," I said. "I have an idea about it."

"All right. Give me your belt."

She hung the machete about her neck and shoved it around to dangle down her back; then she moved onto the ladder and leaned back so that I could make my way clumsily into the space in front of her, with her arms around me. It felt ridiculous, and embarrassing in more ways than one, being held there by a woman, but my hands and feet still weren't much use to me. I would have fallen half a dozen times without her support.

At the bottom, I fumbled my belt back on with tingling fingers, and helped her move the ladder back where it had been. We passed the guard sitting against his rock with his rifle across his knees and his hat over his eyes, motionless, dead. I reminded myself not to underestimate my sexy ally; she wasn't anybody you wanted to turn your back on. We stopped in a sheltered place among the rocks.

She bent over to do something to her feet. "These damn sandals!" she whispered. "I might as well be barefoot."

She straightened up, and we faced each other briefly in

silence. The sky gave enough light that I could see her fairly well. With her blonde hair loose and untidy about her face instead of piled elegantly on her head, without the flashy lipstick and iridescent eye make-up, she was a different person. I was surprised to realize that she was really rather a plain girl.

"Your little friend," Catherine murmured. "She is on top of the cliff with the rifle?"

"Yes."

"Can she really shoot?"

"Don't worry about Sheila," I said. "She'll do her part."

"I'm sure she will. For your sake. Because she loves you. It is very touching."

"Yeah, touching," I said. If women knew how they sounded, sniping at each other, we might have to put up with less static of this kind. "I'll make a deal with you," I said. "The job has developed ramifications. I'll fix von Sachs—Sheila and I—if you'll fix the bird."

"Bird? Oh, the missile." She glanced upstream at the blackness of the cottonwoods. Then she looked at me and smiled. "So that is it. I was wondering if you would really come, when I saw how easily you could shoot him from above. That is why you came?"

"That's it," I said.

"It is nothing to me," she said. "It has nothing to do with my job."

I said, "I've got to sabotage that gadget somehow. Of course Washington would love me to deliver it intact, but they'd rather have it busted than take a chance of losing it again. You take care of it for me and I'll guarantee von Sachs. You get stubborn and I'll go for the missile and you can die heroically doing your goddamn job alone."

She hesitated; then she moved her shoulders in a resigned way. "All right, but how do you expect me to do it? It is such a big thing—"

"The truck," I said. It had taken me a long time to come up with the obvious solution. "I wouldn't know how to gimmick the bird itself, but the control truck is easy. All you have to do is shoot a hole in the gas tank and light a match. I doubt if they have enough electronic talent in this hole to rig up anything that'll fire the missile once that console is a mess of melted wire and plastic." I frowned. "What about the Volkswagen? Who's got the key?"

"It's still in the lock."

"Good. Whichever of us is closest makes for it afterward and picks up the other. Sheila'll be covering us from above, with the rifle. Anything else?"

She hesitated. "Yes. One thing. We are partners here, Henry Evans. But afterward, one day, you will pay for Max. I do not pretend to forgive you."

She turned and went silently back to the tent and slipped inside. I glanced towards the north rim of the canyon. It made me uneasy to know that Sheila's life, as well as mine, was at the mercy of a woman I had no reason to trust, a woman who'd just made a point of reminding me that she owed me something. But there was nothing to be done about it now.

I looked at the machete in my hand and felt the edge. It was a bastard weapon really, too long for a knife, too short for a sword. Well, it would do for what I had in mind. I glanced at my watch. The luminous dial read three thirty-five. I sat down to wait.

At four-thirty it was light enough to start the action. I got up and walked openly towards the tent. A man was building up the fire for breakfast. I saw him stop his work, stare at me, glance up at the cave where I was supposed to be, and reach for a rifle leaning against a nearby tree. I stalked up to the front of the tent, kicked the drugged sentry out of the way, and slashed away the canvas door with a stroke of the machete. I then proceeded to say one of the silliest things I ever said.

"Come on out, Quintana!" I yelled in the quiet dawn. "Come on out and fight like a man!"

XXIII

IT HAD SEEMED reasonable as a theory. Now that I was putting it into practice, it sounded so ridiculous I couldn't believe it would work. I was taking a long chance on a duelling scar a man had picked up in his hotheaded youth, and on that lifelong preoccupation with honor and edged weapons that went with a certain Teutonic mentality, I hoped.

"Come out of there!" I shouted. *"Cobarde! Schweinhund!* Come on out and fight, you slaughterhouse general. What are you stalling for? I suppose you figure if you hide under the bed long enough somebody'll shoot me and save your yellow hide."

It wasn't exactly brilliant invective, particularly since I had to deliver it more or less in Spanish for the sake of the gathering audience. But they were gathering, that was the important thing. They were peering curiously out of the caves and sliding down the ladders and forming a circle around me and the tent. There were several rifles aimed at me as I stood waving my stolen machete dramatically, and the tough little sergeant had come up behind me with his fancy burp-gun, but nobody'd killed me yet.

I called, "Okay, you can relax now, Quintana, and stop shaking. Your boys have me covered. Nobody's going to hurt you. But before you give the word to shoot, let me tell you—"

I told him, in my clumsy Spanish, how his mother was a drunken whore who got impregnated one night by a garbage-eating mongrel dog while lying unconscious in a Berlin gutter. I elaborated on this concept for a while. Then I described his bastard childhood in detail, and went on to tell how he got the scar on his face from a broken beer bottle wielded by a jealous homosexual companion, since everybody knew the Nazis were all fairies; it was a matter of record.

I got a little more fluent as I went along, and out of the corner of my eye I'd catch an occasional faint grin of appreciation. Mexico is a land where the art of vituperation is still respected for its own sake. I was doing okay for a mere gringo. It would be a pity to shoot me while I was affording the camp a certain amount of low-quality entertainment.

One who apparently was not amused, however, was the little sergeant with the machine pistol. I felt his weapon touch me in the back, and I heard the faint click as he released the safety catch.

"That's right, *amigo*," I said over my shoulder. "That is brave and correct. Shoot me in the back. Save your cowardly chief—"

A stir made me look towards the tent again. Von Sachs stood there, buckling on the belt with the machete and the .45 automatic. There was a certain amount of saluting among the men, to which he responded with an impatient outward thrust of his hand. He looked hard and tough in the growing light. If he felt any effects from the beer, and the mickey Catherine had slipped him, he didn't show it.

"What transpires here?" he demanded in Spanish. "Why is this man loose? Why am I awakened by his crazy bellowing? Disarm him!"

I stepped forward before anybody could grab me. "That's right!" I sneered. "That's the way, Quintana! Take the machete away from the terrible man before he cuts somebody! In a camp of men with firearms he must not be allowed to keep his little knife, it is too dangerous!" I threw back my head and spat in his direction. "You've got one of your own, right there on your belt. Why don't *you* take mine away from me? Are you afraid?"

Behind me, the sergeant spoke softly, *"Jefe, con permiso—"* He was asking for permission to shoot.

There was a disapproving murmur from the other men. Von Sachs noted it. There were other things on his mind, of course, like the question of how I came to be standing there free and armed. He wasn't dumb. He glanced quickly towards the tent doorway where Catherine had just appeared, pushing her hair out of her eyes, with her crumpled blouse hanging loose outside her shorts, like an open jacket. Von Sachs spoke quickly, and two men took her by the arms.

"Hold the treacherous slut while I dispose of her accomplice!" He swung back to face me. "So you still wish to die quickly, Mr. Evans. But if I were stupid enough to fight you, I would disappoint you. I would cut you to pieces very slowly."

I grinned scornfully. "You scare me! You and that scar. If it wasn't a beer bottle, it's where you dove through a plate glass window because you were frightened by an American bomb five blocks away."

He hesitated. He knew he was being suckered; he knew he'd be a damn fool to risk everything he'd worked for on the outcome of a crazy duel. And still, there was the matter of a Prussian aristocrat's honor. I'd questioned his courage, I'd cast doubts on the honorable origins of the betraying scar he'd retained through the years of flight and hiding where a sensible man would long since have had it removed by plastic surgery. There was that, and there was the waiting attitude of the men.

The sergeant with the machine pistol spoke quickly behind me: "*Jefe* no! Let me shoot him now!"

For answer, von Sachs grabbed his machete by the hilt and pulled it clear. There wasn't any polite on-guard stuff. He just came for me. Suddenly he was all over me, and he was good. It was all I could do to parry the flashing blade coming at me from all sides.

His men surged aside as I retreated. There were murmurs of approval and gasps of disappointment. It was a weapon they all knew, but they'd probably never seen it used by men who'd trained with foils and sabers. At that, von Sachs had the advantage. He'd learned his stuff with a real weapon. Padded and masked, he'd swung a blade weighing several pounds, sometimes dull for practice, but sometimes, as his face attested, honed and deadly.

I'd done my work with the modern fencing saber, a whippy toy not much heavier than a foil, employing a dainty technique that has little to do with blood and death. As a matter of fact, if you hit hard enough to sting your opponent through his thin canvas jacket, you're scolded for being unsportsmanlike. On the other hand, I did know quite a bit about knives, and I'd done some work with the Japanese fighting stick, a closely related weapon.

He kept coming in, but not as fast as before, and I managed to break up his attack at last and come back at him with a straight-armed lunge that seemed to take him by surprise. He even looked a little disapproving as he beat the point aside and retaliated with a slashing cut to the head, which I parried. I knew I'd learned something, but there wasn't time to analyze it.

I'd weathered the first rush. He'd lost some of his steam, and it was time to think of strategy. It wasn't up to me to skewer him, anyway. I was just the decoy. I started angling my retreat towards the creek bed, well within rifle range of Sheila's position on the north rim.

We were sweating now. The scar was a livid streak on von Sachs' flushed face. I saw Catherine behind him, still held between her guards. That wasn't good, but maybe they'd release her when the shooting started. I didn't look at the canyon wall behind me. Sheila would be there. She'd have been there since the first hint of dawn. I could sense the loaded rifle up there, waiting. I could feel the crosshairs tracking von Sachs as he moved closer, advancing as I retreated.

It made me feel kind of cheap. The man was sincerely trying to kill me in fair fight, and I was just setting him up for a bullet. Well, it's not a chivalrous age, nor is mine an honorable profession. I wasn't about to risk turning loose a wild man with an army and a nuclear missile because of some boyish notions of fair play.

I had it pretty well figured out now. I had to immobilize him for a moment, to make him a stationary target; and I had to get myself completely out of the way so that the chance of my lunging into the bullet wouldn't make Sheila nervous and hasty. I let von Sachs drive me back towards a spot where the almost dry creek bed had a six-foot bank undercut by past floods. I gave ground slowly until I felt the bank start to give; then I let out a despairing cry and jumped back and down, falling in soft sand. That got me out of the line of fire. Six feet above me, von Sachs came to a halt, panting.

He stood there, catching his breath, a beautiful target. I knew a certain regret as I waited for the shot. Good swordsmen are hard to find these days. The regret faded as the shot didn't come.

It was hard to keep from turning my head to look back and up at the rim. Something was wrong up there, terribly wrong, but there wasn't much chance of my seeing the answer from below. I got up slowly, while men crowded to the creek bank on either side of von Sachs, and still the Nazi stood there, machete in hand, and still nothing happened.

It became obvious that nothing was going to happen, presumably because something had already happened to the rifle on the rim or to the small girl behind it.

Catherine's guards had dragged her up to the edge of the wash. Her face told me nothing, but I remembered that she'd wanted von Sachs alive. She'd also said, *One day you will pay for Max. I do not forgive you.*

She was a clever girl. She must have made a deal with somebody; she must have figured out a different solution to her problem, one that gave her revenge as well as success. What it was didn't really matter. Whatever she'd done, or had done, to Sheila, there wasn't much I could do about it at the moment. I could do something about von Sachs, however. She was welcome to him after I got through with him.

"Come on down, grandpa," I called, shaking my machete. "What are you waiting for, the boys to bring a ladder?"

He didn't like the implied sneer at his age. He jumped, going to one knee in the sand. I gave him a break, I let him get to his feet. Then I moved in to kill him.

XXIV

I ALMOST GOT HIM with my first real lunge, and I saw again that little start of surprise and disapproval as he escaped the point with a wild parry that left him open for a cut to the shoulder or face that I passed up. I didn't want to chop him to bits, I just wanted to finish him; and I had the answer now.

It was very simple. He'd never used the point or had it used against him. They fight for the scars and the honor over there; and there's no honor in a scar that starts at the front of the chest and comes out behind. They fight for blood only, not for death. The edge is sharp but the point is blunt. The idea that a man with a cutting weapon in his hand might use it for sticking, too, was not part of his experience. It had probably been outlawed by the rules he'd fought under, to keep them from losing too many students.

I was afraid I'd tipped him off, and I contented myself with slashing and chopping for a while, carrying the fight to him. The sand made it tough for both of us, but his legs were older than mine. He fought cunningly and defensively, however, giving ground upstream past the cottonwoods and the missile, sparing himself for another major effort. Then it came, and he drove me back with a flashing attack, turned, and ran for the bank, shelving here.

He held that rise for a minute or two. I couldn't drive him off it, but I could work my way upstream to where there was no longer any bank to amount to anything. There were no shots from above. There was no sign of life at the top of the cliff. I should have left her in Tucson, I thought. She'd be safe now.

Von Sachs almost took my head off with a savage cut. The parry jarred the machete in my hand. It was no time for regrets. We were in the cottonwoods, fighting at the base of the Rudovic III, slugging it out with ancient tools and techniques in the shadow of the weapon of the future.

He was tiring. I had him now, and I looked towards Catherine so she'd know I was making her a present of him. If I'd had any doubts of her treachery—whatever the details might be—the fact that she was standing alone, unguarded, but making no effort to run for the truck as we'd arranged, would have convicted her. Her guards had forgotten all about her, seeing their *jefe* driven back. The men watching were all silent now. There would be a kind of sigh when a weapon failed to reach the mark, that was all.

I went in for the head, let von Sachs break up my attack, and gave him an opening. He was slow in taking advantage of it, but he came along nicely at last, and I teased him by retreating, and still he came, and I let myself falter as if my foot had slipped. I let my weapon swing wide as I caught myself. I heard the sigh of the men, and I saw the light come back into the German's eyes, and his machete made a whistling sound as he changed his attack from left to right to take advantage of the unguarded side.

In the middle of his cutover, while his hand was still high, I lunged, driving the point in hard and straight. He was coming to meet it. The blade went in clean and didn't stop until the hilt was against his shirt.

I heard the groan of the men. I saw von Sachs' face change and die. The machete dropped from his hand. I braced myself and pulled my own weapon free. As he fell towards me, I caught him and got the pistol from his holster left-handed. Then I was standing at the base of the missile with the bloody machete in one hand and the cocked automatic in the other, facing the leaderless army that had been going to conquer an empire, for all the world like Errol Flynn playing Custer's Last Stand, or something.

It took them a moment to make up their minds. I noticed that Catherine was missing. Looking over the heads of the crowd I saw her stealing away downhill. When she realized she was away clear, she started to run. For a girl, she ran very well.

I wasn't at all sure what she was up to, but I held the picture in my mind as something nice to die with, and shot a man in the face as he came in to split me in two. I shot the next one in the chest so close it scorched his shirt, and I pushed the machete into a third, and they fell back, but only for a moment. They were all yelling now. They came in again and I emptied the .45 into them and swung the machete like a scythe, using both hands, hacking and slashing to keep them off me.

Down the canyon, I was vaguely aware, something was adding to the general confusion by making a raucous, squawking noise, like a raven with the croup. It meant nothing to me. I was just trying to stay alive for another second or two, although it was beginning to seem hardly worth the effort. I lost the machete and went down on one knee, and a familiar figure loomed up out of the melee: the tough little sergeant. He drove the butt of his machine pistol at my head, and I caught the weapon and yanked him down and got my hands on his throat and dug my thumbs in where they'd do the most good, or harm.

He took a little while to die. I scrambled for the squirt-gun he'd dropped and pointed it in a general outward direction and pulled the trigger and rose, spraying the weapon like a hose, only to discover I was shooting at nothing at all. They were all running, and I was coughing, and smoke was curling out from under the bird against which I stood, and I could hear the hissing sound of the engines warming up. The damn thing was about to blast off. The squawking down the valley, I realized at last, was the warning siren of the control truck. . . .

I ran for the creek. Behind me, the Rudovic had begun to whistle like a tea kettle; there was a funny sort of earthquake vibration. I leaped down into the wash and threw myself back under the overhanging bank, drew three long breaths, buried my face in my arms, and closed my eyes.

The canyon was full of thunder. Part of the bank shook loose and fell on top of me. There was a moment of intense heat, as if a giant blowtorch were playing on the dirt that covered me. Gradually the heat and noise died away. I suppose I should have waited a discreet interval for the fumes to disperse, but I wasn't quite sure I wasn't buried alive, and it made me panicky.

When I came out of my shallow grave, I got a lungful of chemical fumes that set me coughing again. The stuff was all around me like a fog. I climbed up the bank where it had crumbled, and sunlight hit me on the shoulders, although I was still standing in white smoke to the shoulders. It occurred to me to look up and there was the bird, a small, gleaming, splinter in the blue sky at the end of a long, arching white trail of smoke.

The rocket engines were still firing, I saw. Pretty soon they would cut out and leave the missile to follow its trajectory to the target. El Paso, von Sachs had said. Nothing could stop it now, I thought; and then there was a silent puff of smoke up there, and the tiny pencil of death broke up into a graceful rain of fragments. Belatedly, the sound of the explosion that had destroyed it hit me like a clap of thunder. I couldn't help ducking although it was obvious that the nearest piece was going to hit miles away.

The Volkswagen was a bit scorched, but it had been out of the area of the direct rocket blast. None of the dazed men wandering around made any attempt to interfere as I started the little car and drove down the canyon to the control truck. Catherine appeared at the door of the cab, and made her way over to me, limping as if her feet hurt. She still hadn't managed to get her blouse buttoned. Von Sachs would have got an eyeful, had he been alive. I didn't give a damn, and neither, apparently, did she.

She got in and slumped wearily in the seat beside me. There was a little pistol in her hand.

"It was one of the bearded technicians," she said. "One ran but the other hit the firing button before I could shoot. Luckily the other button was marked. The one to destroy it."

"Sure," I said. Smoke was curling out of the truck. As I watched, the whole vehicle burst into flames. "That wasn't necessary, now," I said.

Her voice was dull and tired. "You said to burn it."

"So I did. Give me the gun." I held out my hand. After a moment she put her automatic into it. Just what part she'd played still wasn't exactly clear to me, but I said, "If you sold out Sheila, I'm going to kill you."

Catherine glanced at me quickly but didn't speak. I put the car into gear and drove on down the canyon. The firing of the missile and apparently drawn off any sentries stationed along the trail. We met no one. Emerging from Copala Canyon we crossed the open valley beyond, parked the car out of sight, and went on foot to where Sheila and I had cached the luggage. It was still there, undisturbed.

Something else was there, too. I walked forward slowly, looking at the small figure huddled against a rock. Hearing me approach, Sheila looked up. Her face was scratched and dirty and streaked with tears. She'd apparently run hard and heedlessly to get here so fast; her hands were cut from falls and the knees of her pants were torn.

"I couldn't do it," she whispered. "I had him in the sights. My finger was on the trigger. It was a beautiful, easy shot, like on the target range. But I simply couldn't do it!"

"Sure," I said. "That's what happened in Costa Verde, isn't it? You didn't have any trouble with the grip safety of El Fuerte's automatic. You simply couldn't bring yourself to shoot him."

I should have known, of course. I remembered another time she should have shot and hadn't. There was nothing to be bitter about. It's a well-recognized phenomenon. It has nothing to do with marksmanship. Half the boys in Korea never fired their weapons in combat or fired to miss. Of course she might have told me, but to hell with that.

I said, "Well, some people can kill people and some people can't. It looks like you're just in the wrong line of business, Skinny."

"Eric, I—"

"Think nothing of it," I said. I hoped my voice sounded nice and reasonable. "Everything worked out swell anyway, doll. Let's get out of here before the road fills up with ex-empire-builders going back to their farms. . . ."

XXV

WHEN I GOT BACK to Tucson some days later, having disposed of my passengers and made my preliminary report along the way, there was a long package awaiting me in the motel office. I took it to my room and opened it, finding a long plastic case inside. Within the case was a rifle I recognized, much more solid and businesslike than the light sporter we'd taken into Mexico. There was also a note: THANK YOU FOR THE LOAN. PRESIDENT AVILA WAS MUCH IMPRESSED. JIMINEZ.

I frowned at this briefly; then I went out to a pay phone and called Washington. There was no delay in getting Mac on the line.

"Did you receive a package we forwarded after inspection?" he asked.

"Yes, sir. The meaning escapes me, for the moment."

"Then you haven't seen the papers."

"Not for a day or two."

"The president of Costa Verde was assassinated last weekend by a hidden marksman operating at extreme range. There is now a reform government headed by Colonel Hector Jiminez."

I looked at the sunlit Tucson street outside the booth, but I remembered a jungle clearing at night, and a jaunty little man with a big cigar saying, *If one has the firearms one can always find men to use them.*

I said, "Well, I told you Hector's compassion was very interesting, sir."

"Some people here in Washington are upset. They had arrangements with Avila."

"I feel for them, deeply," I said. "It's very inconsiderate of these lousy little Latin countries to go reforming their governments and inconveniencing people, just as if they were sovereign nations or something."

Mac said, "They are also upset about the fate of a certain large item of armament. They feel that, so close to the border, it might have been preserved for examination. They feel, in other words, that perhaps its destruction was a little hasty."

I drew a long breath. "Yes, sir," I said. "Hasty."

"I thought you'd like to know that our country appreciates our efforts, as always, Eric."

"Yes, sir," I said. For some reason I found myself grinning. Perhaps it was the tone of his voice. "Yes, sir. As always."

After that there was the usual business of cleaning things up officially, which took several more days. One evening I came back to my motel room to find Catherine Smith waiting for me. It was the first time I'd seen her since we'd parted just north of the border, but I'd done considerable thinking about her, and some research, while writing up my final reports.

There wasn't any doubt what she was there for. Her street clothes were neatly hung over a chair in the corner. She was dressed exactly as I'd seen her first, in the ruffly black negligee and the high-heeled mules and the other stuff designed for male appreciation. There were two stemmed glasses on the dresser. A bucket of ice held a couple of interesting bottles.

The whole thing was so obvious it was kind of nice, if you know what I mean: I was so clearly meant to understand that we had some unfinished business to attend to, business that had once been interrupted by Max's hypodermic needle.

I said, "I won't ask how you got in."

She smiled. I remembered that I'd thought her face rather plain without make-up, but it wasn't plain tonight. Smiling, she came close to being beautiful, in an intriguing, off-beat sort of way.

"I hope you like sparkling Burgundy," she said. "One gets tired of champagne. How is the little girl with the tender heart? You know of course why she never confessed her weakness to you. She was afraid you would despise her. I am very much afraid she loved you, Mr. Evans."

I said, "Why would that concern you?"

"Because you've sent her away, haven't you? To lead a life more suitable for tender-hearted little girls?"

I said, rather stiffly, "Well, she obviously has no place in this work. It was time to ease her out before she got herself and a lot of other people killed."

"And you are not going to see her again, are you? Because deep down inside you are aware, no matter what excuses you made for her, that no woman can love a man very much if she won't kill for him. That isn't real love, the kind we know, is it, Mr. Evans? But still, you are feeling sad and lonely, which is nice. It will make you appreciate me more. Now you may open the wine. . . ."

In the morning she was still asleep when I came back to the room with coffee—asleep or pretending. With her, it wasn't safe to jump to conclusions. Anyway, she let me have a good look at her lying on the big rumpled bed, nude except for the sheer black stockings that, unsupported and forgotten, had slipped below her knees. They made her look like a naughty photograph.

When I kicked the door shut behind me, she rolled over, stretched luxuriously, and opened her eyes to look at me.

"Coffee is served, ma'am," I said. I grinned. "Damn if you aren't the most pornographic-looking woman I ever spent the night with."

She laughed. "I try very hard. It is nice of you to say that I am successful."

She sat up and discovered the untidy stockings and pulled them up for inspection. It had been a long, rough night and the nylons were hardly, let's say, in mint condition. She wrinkled her nose at them, stripped the wreckage off her legs, dropped it into the wastebasket, and picked her ruffled negligee off the floor. She shook it out dubiously, found it undamaged, and with dignity brought it over for me to hold for her, as if it were a sable wrap and she were in diamonds and evening dress instead of stark naked.

I set the coffee aside and obliged. After tying the little bow at the throat, she tilted her face up to be kissed. I performed this service also.

She said a little breathlessly, "It was the damn sword."

"What was?"

"The reason I came. One reason I came. You have been wondering, haven't you?"

"Well, the question did cross my mind."

"A man with a rifle or pistol, bah!" she said. "What is that but a machine with a machine? Bang, bang, bang. But a man with a sword. . . . It was so beautiful, that fight. I forgot what you'd asked me to do, watching. The sunlight on the blades, the two men, the precise movements, so formal, like a ritual, like a dance of death. And then the lunge, like lightning from the sky. You could have walked over and taken me then, right there in the dust in front of all those men."

I said, "Life is just one lost opportunity after another, Vadya." She started and looked at me sharply. I said, "Drink your coffee. Your plane ticket is on the dresser."

She licked her lips. "What name did you use?"

I said, "There's a list we have. We call it the high-priority list. There was a man named Martell on it, for instance, but he died in the mountains in New Mexico, so we checked him off. There are some other men, but they haven't been checked off yet, so the names are classified. And then there are the women, including a mysterious lady called Vadya, very dangerous. The descriptions we have are not at all consistent. Sometimes she is described as enchantingly lovely, sometimes as dumpy and plain. Sometimes she is blonde, sometimes brunette. Even the color of her eyes changes. That can be done with contact lenses, you know. Mostly they are blue, however. I have read some very lyrical descriptions of Vadya's eyes. There are also some fingerprints on record."

She licked her lips again, watching me. "I see."

"The prints on the outside of your little gun were badly smeared," I said, "but we got a very good impression off the clip. You weren't interested in von Sachs at all, dead or alive, were you, Vadya? That was just one of your tricks of misdirection. It was the missile all the time, wasn't it? You killed the technician, you fired it, and then you destroyed it in flight. And set fire to the truck. A thorough job."

She reached for the paper cup of coffee, looked at it, hesitated, and looked at me. She shrugged as if to say that if I wanted to poison her, now that I had found her out, so be it. She drank, and nodded.

"Of course. We could not have a Rudovic in the hands of an irresponsible fascist, and we certainly didn't want your country to get it. It had to be destroyed." She glanced at me almost shyly. "Did you say there was a ticket?"

"To Mexico City. You have about forty-five minutes to dress and reach the airport. I'll drive you."

She said, drawing a long breath, "I'm disappointed in you, my dear. You are being sentimental again. You should kill me."

"I know," I said. "And I'll probably regret this, but there's been enough killing. I have permission to do it this way."

She said, "We have our lists, too. There is a man on several of them. A tall man responsible for the death of one Martell. For the death of one Caselius. For the death of one Tina, and others. And now for the death of Max. There are many black marks against you over there, Eric, also known as Matthew Helm."

I grinned. "It wasn't entirely admiration that drew you here, then?"

"No. After making my report, I received new instructions a few days ago."

I said, "Sure. I wasn't certain I'd wake up this morning. But I guess you've got a little sentimentality, too. Enough not to spoil a pleasant reunion between two old comrades in arms. I was kind of gambling on that."

She looked at me for a moment longer with an expression I couldn't read. Then she laughed and turned to dress. At the airport we stopped at the gate. I put into her hand the little travel case she'd brought to my room.

"Goodbye, Eric," she said. "Under the circumstances, I hope we never meet again. At least . . . I think I do."

As I watched her walk out to the waiting plane, I wasn't quite sure how I felt about it, either.